SHW

ALLEN COUNTY PUBLIC

3 1833 03778 0100

P9-BIL-771

"I LOVE IT!" J.D. HOLLERED.

All his life J.D. had dreamed of something like this happening to him. He was a dinosaur. A *dinosaur*!

He could go where he wanted. Do what he wanted. No one could stop him.

J.D. looked around the green valley and saw another dinosaur lapping water from a puddle.

It looked like a T. rex, only bigger, with jaws that reminded J.D. of a pair of scissors.

The dinosaur's head swiveled. Muddy water splashed as it fixed J.D. with its dark eyes.

"Hey, Ugly," called J.D., his words transformed into a growl, "what are you lookin' at?"

J.D.'s heart skipped a beat as Ugly rushed toward him. He hadn't expected Ugly to move so fast. Or to be so *big*.

"You want a fight!" J.D. cried. "You came to the right guy. I may be little. But one thing I've *never* been is defenseless!"

Lexile:

LSU ☑yes
SJB ☐yes
BL: 4.7
Pts: 5

Long before the universe was ours...
it was *theirs!*

**Read all the
DINOVERSE adventures
by Scott Ciencin**

BEVERLY HILLS BRONTOSAURUS

by Scott Ciencin

illustrated by Mike Fredericks

Random House 🏠 New York

To my beloved wife, Denise,
who taught me that the future belongs to those
who believe in the beauty of their dreams.
—S.C.

Text copyright © 2000 by Scott Ciencin
Interior illustrations copyright © 2000 by Mike Fredericks
Cover art copyright © 2000 by Adrian Chesterman

All rights reserved under International and Pan-American Copyright
Conventions. Published in the United States by Random House, Inc., New York,
and simultaneously in Canada by Random House of Canada Limited, Toronto.

www.randomhouse.com/kids

Library of Congress Catalog Card Number: 00-103220
ISBN: 0-375-80595-8
RL: 5.5

Printed in the United States of America   September 2000
10 9 8 7 6 5 4 3 2 1
RANDOM HOUSE and colophon are registered
trademarks of Random House, Inc.

• A NOTE FROM THE AUTHOR •

Dear Reader,

Welcome to Book #5 of DINOVERSE!

If you've read the first four books in this series, you've already seen Bertram Phillips's weird science fair project in action. The device zapped the minds of Bertram and three other Wetherford Junior High students back in time and into the bodies of dinosaurs.

Bertram and his friends had some wild adventures before returning to the present. But the story was far from over. Bertram's science teacher, Mr. London, found a way to make the M.I.N.D. Machine work again. Now Bertram and a dozen other students are trapped in prehistoric California, and the fates of two worlds depend on their actions.

Facing fiery volcanoes, lakes of acid, and fearsome predators, Bertram is forced to rely on one of the baddest predators he knows—fellow student J.D. "Judgment Day" Harms.

Will J.D. help Bertram save the future—or will he destroy it?

You may wonder if the age of dinosaurs was anything like what you're reading about in the DINOVERSE books. According to the fossil record, it very likely was. How did the dinosaurs live? What did they eat? What about the weather and landscape? All of those questions have crossed the minds of scientists. And the fossil record has given the answers to them, to me, and now to *you*.

So come back with me to a time when the world belonged not to humans but to the most magnificent creatures the Earth has ever known.

Scott Ciencin

PROLOGUE

Wetherford, Montana
Late May, Two Hours and Fifty-one Minutes to
Temporal-Spatial Implosion

Aaron Aimes woke with a start. His alarm clock was blaring, and a *dinosaur* was sitting on his chest. A Compsognathus, to be precise.

It was turkey-sized, with small two-fingered hands and a wild beak filled with sharp teeth.

Aaron sighed.

He could handle the dinosaur. It was paisley and it was stuffed—someone's idea of a joke. An attached note read: *Come on, Aaron, don't be a big turkey. Get out of bed!*

The easy-listening music cranked up to full volume was a whole other deal. He reached over and gave the clock radio a shove. It fell to the floor, but its electrical cord didn't pop out of the wall the way it should have.

Aaron craned his neck a little to see that an extension cord had been attached to the plug. There had been no extension cord when he went to bed. And Cory the compie had been on an upper shelf in his closet.

What was going on?

Making a face, Aaron stumbled to his feet, and the stuffed dinosaur rolled to the floor. He brushed his long blond hair out of his eyes and crouched down to turn off the radio.

Silence washed over him. It was wonderful. Now he could get back to sleep.

Sure, there was a mystery here. He had questions. But they could wait.

He had the covers halfway up when the door to his room burst open and a woman he had never seen before entered.

"Hey!" Aaron hollered. He was wearing only his boxers.

"Hey yourself," the woman replied. "Get out of bed. You have school today."

Aaron felt a sudden panic.

"Who are you? And where's Mrs. Greenleaf?" Aaron asked. An image of the housekeeper appeared in his mind. She was dark-haired. Fiftyish. Sweet with round cheeks. Grandmotherly. And, *most important*, a pushover.

Come on, Mrs. Greenleaf! Aaron recalled telling her

last week. *You know I've been dying to put in my first day at Wetherford Junior High ever since Dad and I moved here, but I don't feel well. And I don't want to be spewing up chunks of breakfast and getting everybody sick.*

That had been over a week ago. Aaron had come up with three more excellent excuses since then.

Mrs. Greenleaf had bought them all.

Then something weird had happened at the school. Some kind of electrical disaster or something, with a bunch of students getting zapped, and one teacher, too.

See, Mrs. Greenleaf? Good thing I wasn't in school that day!

And today, well, if the sick thing didn't work, he could just say he didn't think it was safe. *I heard on the radio that since this is the first day that the school's officially open again, a whole week after that other thing happened, lots of parents are keeping their kids home until they know it's safe over there. You want me to be safe, don't you?*

Aaron loved Mrs. Greenleaf. He also loved sleeping. And pizza. And Doritos. And DVDs.

That, pretty much, was his life. And surfing and rollerblading. And dreaming of doing a guest spot on a Pamela Anderson Lee TV show someday.

Of course, surfing and the guest spot were pretty much out now that his dad had been moved from the military base in California to the one here in Montana.

This woman was no Mrs. Greenleaf. She was tall, blond, and thin. Early forties. Decked out in a navy blue business suit. Probably someone his dad knew through the army.

Scary.

"I'm Maria. Your *new* housekeeper and personal trainer."

Aaron looked down at his muscled chest. "I don't need—"

"Not that kind of personal trainer. Consider me more of a lifestyle adjuster. Slackers are my specialty. Tell me, what is it you want out of life, Aaron?"

"To *sleep*!"

"That's an interesting want. Aboriginal tribesmen consider the dreaming world as real as the waking world. They feel wisdom and spiritual guidance come from that other place beyond our normal reality."

Aaron gasped as Maria bent down and performed an act of either bravery or complete stupidity: She picked up his discarded jeans and T-shirt. She kept them away from her nose as she tossed them at the thirteen-year-old.

"You're not an Aborigine. Get dressed. *Now*. If I have to come back to get you, I'll be angry. You wouldn't like me when I'm angry."

Maria left the room. Aaron shook his head, saluted

to the closed door, and looked mournfully around his room. He had it just the way he liked it: his surfboard up against the bookcase, pictures of the friends he had made at his last eight schools over the last two years on the wall, and his rollerblades, comic books, CDs, DVDs, and other stuff cluttering the floor.

It would all be put away when he got home. Ravaged by a reorganizing monster! He stopped before the stuffed dinosaur.

"Any tips for dealing with predators?" he asked.

Cory the compie was silent.

Downstairs, Maria rushed Aaron through breakfast, then hurried him out to the garage, where the Ford Explorer waited. They bulleted through traffic, Aaron desperately attempting to come up with some excuse this woman might buy. It wasn't that he hated school or anything. He just had a motto, that's all. In fact, it was printed on the T-shirt he was wearing: *Why put off till tomorrow what you can put off forever?*

The Explorer stopped before the three-story brick junior high with a screech of brakes.

Maria pushed down her designer shades so that she could peer over the top. "You're a military brat. If I tell you to meet me *here* at fifteen hundred hours, you'll understand, right?"

Aaron had to stifle a smile. He knew how to play this one. Say yes, then later say what he *thought* she'd meant—

"That's three P.M.," Maria said. "On the dot. Understand?"

Aaron frowned, his plan blown. "Are you sure my dad knows about this?"

"He called me personally. Now move."

Aaron moved. He hauled his backpack out of the car, amazed that Ms. Attila the Hun hadn't wanted to rummage through it. Well, at least it showed she was human and could make a mistake. He patted the bag with a small smile.

Approaching the school cautiously, he saw that some students were gathered in little cliques on the lawn. Others stayed together in clusters near the main doors. A few stood by a gigantic statue of a T. rex.

That's right! realized Aaron. His dad had told him that almost everyone at this school was really into dinosaurs. One guy even wrote stories about them that were published each month in some big magazine. And Aaron didn't question Colonel Charmin when he mentioned something like that.

"That's 'Colonel Charmin, *sir*' to you!" his dad would tease him. Aaron had given him the nickname because, despite his chiseled jaw, cold blue eyes, and iron-man build, the guy was a big softie.

Of course, neither of them had been exactly the same since his mom died in the accident. Not his dad, who hadn't been able to pull her out of the wreck, and not Aaron, who had been trapped beside her for hours.

He swallowed uneasily. Coming to a new place always brought back the past, and that was the last thing he wanted to think about. His mom had loved them both, and they missed her a lot. Life had become about work and play—his dad worked all the time, and he played as much as possible. And that was about all.

Aaron studied the school building. It didn't look too bad. Kind of old-fashioned, and that was nice.

He swung his bag around and unzipped it. "Time for one last roundup!"

His rollerblades were in the bag. He sat on the lawn and put them on, then got up and went gliding.

Immediately Aaron captured the attention of almost every student on the lawn. He skated down the main walkway, nodding at the pretty girls and ignoring the jocks who shook their heads at having another slacker in their midst.

Then he heard a soft, warm laugh that immediately arrested his attention. He turned his head and saw a pretty girl, about thirteen, grinning broadly. She had short-cut blond hair and the stunning features of a storybook princess. Her white dress reached to her knees, the skirt fluttering slightly in the early morning breeze. She met Aaron's eyes and mouthed the words, "Cool T-shirt."

Whoa.

Aaron was only barely aware of all the other students gathered around the young woman. He saw angry, protective glares from guys and narrow, disapproving stares from the blonde's girlfriends. He took in jackets with school letters, hunched shoulders, and crew cuts. Very little of it had any impact on Aaron. The grinning blonde was all that mattered.

A voice whispered in his mind: *Don't get attached. Don't start liking anyone too much. You never know how long we'll be in any one place, and I wouldn't want to see you hurt.*

The voice of Colonel Charmin was coming in loud and clear. A voice that was being ignored.

The world sailed by, and Aaron strained to keep the pretty blonde, the picture-perfect princess, in view.

Then another voice was calling to him, and this one wasn't in his head.

"Look out!"

He didn't look out. His gaze remained on the princess. Mistake. *Big* mistake.

Aaron watched the princess's expression change. Her grin faded and her brown eyes went wide with alarm.

Then Aaron hit a wall.

Only it wasn't an ordinary wall. *This* wall grunted and went down hard, hauling Aaron with it.

This wall also smelled of sweat, leather, denim,

aftershave, and grease. And this wall used language that would have made the colonel's lifelong army buddies take notes.

All around Aaron, students were laughing.

"Ow!" Aaron hollered as his head hit the pavement. He hadn't worn his helmet or pads, just his blades. He rolled away from the Wall and settled on his back.

A circle of students crowded around him. Aaron could only barely make out their faces because of the bright morning sunlight.

Aaron sat up a little and saw the princess among the onlookers. Then he heard an angry growl from the ground, a few feet beyond the ring of spectators.

"Come on, Claire," said a guy with short-cropped red hair and a Wetherford football jersey. He took her arm. "You don't want to be around for this."

Claire. The princess's name was Claire.

She frowned. "But—"

Then a roar sounded, and the crowd parted. Aaron felt a little woozy, but he struggled to his feet anyway—just in time to get his first full look at the Wall.

The guy was enormous. He was taller than any eighth-grader Aaron had ever seen. He wore a black leather jacket with a torn gray T-shirt beneath, denim jeans, and leather boots with shiny silver tips.

He had *no* neck. He was a towering slab of anger,

frustration, and muscle. His hair was short and dark. His eyes were deep black, impenetrable wells. He was already *shaving* and had stubble on his meaty cheeks and bucket chin.

He looked as if he should have had smoke pouring out of his flaring nostrils.

Standing in this guy's path reminded Aaron of the day when he and his father had stood on the peak of a great mountain, facing winds that tore at them and threatened to flick them off into nothingness.

"Who do you think you are?" the Wall asked.

Aaron rubbed his forehead and looked around for Claire. "Hey, chill, okay? I didn't see you."

He didn't see Claire, either. She had been led away by one of her protectors. What he *did* see was Ms. Attila the Hun driving away in the Explorer. Aaron had a sudden crazy notion that she'd *known* what was going to happen, and that was why she let him pack his blades.

A huge, meaty hand appeared before Aaron's long, angular face and gripped his cheeks and jaw like a vise. Aaron's field of vision changed as the Wall forced Aaron to look at him.

"Someone tell me this reject didn't just say what I thought he did," the Wall demanded.

No one spoke.

"You're telling *me* to chill? *Me?* Do you have any idea who I am?"

3 1833 03778 0100

Aaron didn't—and he didn't want to, either. "Leggo."

The vise tightened.

"You are so dead," the Wall said.

Aaron reacted without thinking. His hand went up and closed around the Wall's little finger. He bent it back hard and fast.

"Arrrrhhhh!" shouted the Wall, instantly letting Aaron go. The crowd gasped.

"Let's just forget it," Aaron said. "I'm sorry."

The fist came at Aaron so quickly that it was nearly a blur. He dodged it, to the awed whispers of the crowd. Then Aaron toppled from his feet, the blades throwing off his balance. The Wall was on him, huge hands grasping Aaron's shirt, when a voice rang out. A *teacher's* voice.

"Mr. Harms! Let him go."

The Wall tensed, then opened his hands. Aaron sank back to the pavement and saw a tall, thin man in a dark suit approach. The man had hawklike features and wore a brightly colored tie.

"Now step away and report to the principal's office. I'll meet you there in a minute."

"He started it," the Wall said. He stood up and stepped away from Aaron. Then he wiggled his little finger. "*That* is going to cost ya."

"Enough, J.D.," the man said. "Go."

"I hear and obey, O master," the Wall said.

"Besides, time's on *my* side."

Aaron rolled back, feeling a little less steady than before.

"Look out," a soft voice said from behind. Aaron whirled, nearly falling again. A hand shot out to steady him. A short girl with black hair stood before him. She wore a T-shirt, blue jeans, and black leather boots.

She nodded to the man who had sent J.D. to the principal's office. "It's okay, Mr. L. I'll get Slick here to the nurse."

The man smiled and walked off.

"That's Mr. London," the dark-haired girl said. "Science teacher. He's cool."

The first bell rang. The lawn cleared quickly. The dark-haired girl led Aaron to the front steps and sat him down. She touched his forehead.

"Does this hurt?" she asked.

He shrugged.

"Okay, you'll live. Anyway, I'm Janine Farehouse," she said. "I'll take you to the nurse, like I said. But first we need to talk."

One Hour and Eleven Minutes to
Temporal-Spatial Implosion

Aaron sat in third-period English thinking about all that had happened to him this morning—and all he had learned. He had a window seat and found himself looking out at the school's front lawn and the enormous dinosaur statue that adorned it.

The guy from his grade who had gotten some of his dinosaur stories published was at the front of the class, answering questions about what he had done and how he had made his first sale. His name was Bernie. Or Benjamin. Something like that. Aaron really hadn't been paying attention.

On the other hand, a lot of students had been paying attention to *Aaron* this morning. He was used to the normal scrutiny the new guy in class would get. But this was something different. Students whispered. Pointed. One of them showed another the move Aaron's dad had taught him, the one he had used on J.D. earlier.

He had passed Claire twice in the hall. She had tried to approach him, but other students had intercepted her, leading her away. She'd almost bumped into a pretty but tough-looking black-haired girl in a black leather miniskirt. Someone said her name was Holly Cronk, and she looked like pure attitude on two real nice legs. But Claire was the girl for him.

Aaron glanced back to the student doing the guest lecture while the teacher, Mrs. Stonebreaker, graded papers. The guy wore glasses and had dark hair. He was also pretty bulked up, wearing jeans and a tight black T-shirt to show off his arms.

"Brains and a bod," a cute brunette said from two seats behind Aaron. "Candayce Chambers doesn't know how lucky she is."

"And he's nice, too," another girl said.

"Shut up, you're making me sick."

From the front, the young guy said, "That's everything. The rest of the period is for study. Thanks."

He smiled as he was given a round of applause, then he took a seat next to Aaron.

"Hey," the guy said, "I spoke with Janine."

That caught Aaron's attention. He shook the guy's outstretched hand. "Yeah, you're the dino dude."

"Whatever," the guy said. "My name's Bertram Phillips."

"Right," Aaron said. He repeated Bertram's name three times in his head, making sure he wouldn't forget this time.

"Listen," said Bertram, "I heard about what happened with Judgment Day."

Aaron straightened up in his seat. "Judgment Day? That's what people call him?"

"I thought Janine would have told you."

"No. She didn't."

Bertram's expression became grave. "I don't like being the one to give out bad news or anything, but...have you heard about eighth-period lunch?"

Aaron shook his head.

"Everyone's calling it the WJH Slacker Smackdown.

J.D. got hold of your schedule. I think you can guess the rest."

Aaron's shoulders slumped. "So everything Janine said about this guy is for real."

"J.D.'s a hard case. He hangs kids up by their ankles and shakes their lunch money out of them. He busts things up. He busts *people* up. But, um, there might be a way to get you off the hook."

Aaron leaned in closer. "I'm listening."

"How much do you know about dinosaurs?" Bertram asked.

"I've got a compie at home. He's stuffed. Had him since I was a kid. My favorite dino. Everybody's got one, right?"

Bertram sighed and ran his hand through his hair. "Right. Okay, Dino 101. Predator dinosaurs: big bodies, tiny brains. Not a lot of memory. If you went back to the nurse, said your head hurt, you were feeling dizzy, whatever, she'd send you home. Guaranteed. The school doesn't want to risk any liability. I spoke with a friend of mine named Will, and we figured we could think of something else to help take J.D.'s mind off what happened this morning."

"It was an accident."

"You ran him over. Everyone laughed. Then you did the pinkie lock or whatever. Trust me, it's not good. Will and I can come up with something else to occupy J.D. Believe me, we've both had a lot of experience dealing with predators."

Aaron's shoulders slumped. He knew Bertram was giving him good advice, and he knew he should take it, no question. For as long as he could remember, or at least ever since the accident, whenever people had offered him an easy out, he'd been more than willing to take it.

But something was different today. Something he couldn't quite put his finger on.

"What's the matter?" asked Bertram. "You don't like the plan? Or is it...Oh, I get it. What's her name?"

Aaron laughed softly. "No, it's not like that."

"You don't want some girl to think you can't take care of yourself, right?"

Aaron frowned. "Okay, it is like that."

"So what's her name?"

"Claire DeLacey."

Bertram sat back and sighed. "Claire. Wow. Yeah, I see the problem."

So could Aaron.

Janine had already told Aaron all about "Crystal" Claire. She was considered a treasure around Wetherford Junior High. A pure, perfect ray of light, a soft, sweet, fragile young thing that *no one* wanted to see hurt in any way.

Claire was always picked for the leads in the school plays. She sang at shows and at church. She had never been exposed to anything bad in her life, and everyone wanted things to stay that way.

"By the way, who's the guy with the red hair and the crew cut? He has on a football jersey today," Aaron asked. "Is he—"

Bertram shook his head. "Reggie Firth. Not her boyfriend. He just enjoys acting like he is."

"Cool!" Aaron glanced at the window and saw the morning sunlight sparkling off the metal statue of the giant T. rex outside. "Listen, I don't want to seem ungrateful or anything, but..."

"You want to know why I'm helping you."

Aaron shrugged and looked back at Bertram. "You don't even know me."

"Have you read any of my stuff?"

Aaron felt embarrassed that he hadn't. He scratched his head, trying to recall what Janine had told him.

"Uh...there's, like, this machine and it sends these eighth-graders back in time and they become dinosaurs and stuff. Right?"

"Yeah, pretty much. My dad's a paleontologist. We kind of work on the stories together. It's fun. The thing is, I've been through some stuff, and I've learned not to judge people. Everyone's got sides to themselves that they don't want people to see, or they're afraid of people seeing. I figure that's the way it is with you and J.D., and if Will and I can keep this thing between the two of you from getting any worse, then we should. It's that simple."

Aaron had a hard time picturing a warm, sensitive side to J.D. "Judgment Day" Harms, but he kept silent.

"But what about Claire?" Aaron asked.

"First things first. Getting into a fight isn't the way to convince her or her folks to let you take her to the graduation dance."

"I was just thinking pizza and a movie."

"Whatever. First things first, okay? The one thing I know is that we've got time. The trick is using it wisely."

Three Minutes and Seventeen Seconds to Temporal-Spatial Implosion

Aaron had no idea why, but he'd been putting off going to the nurse's office for more than an hour. He'd suffered through classes that were completely meaningless to him, considering that he was so close to the end of the school year.

This had happened to him last year, too. He wouldn't have to take finals; he wouldn't be expected to join any teams or even do much of anything in gym. He'd do a couple of easy assignments, and that would be his grade. No biggie.

Now he was at his locker between periods, and he

couldn't even *remember* what class he'd been to last. History, probably. Exactly what *he* would be if he didn't get out of school in a hurry.

The best part was that if the nurse phoned Ms. Attila the Hun and she refused to come get him, or, even better, she wasn't there, and his dad had to come over from the base—that would be it for her. He'd have Mrs. Greenleaf back in a heartbeat.

So why couldn't he get excited at the prospect? Pizza! Doritos! DVDs!

Sleep!

He saw the door to the nurse's office down the hall—and he saw Claire. She stood by herself for once, near an open locker. A note was in her hand, and she laughed as she read it.

That laugh...

He couldn't say why, but for some reason, her laugh made him feel something deep inside that he hadn't felt in years.

This is crazy, he thought. *Colonel Charmin would never approve.*

He didn't know this girl. He'd never even exchanged so much as a sentence with her. She'd liked his T-shirt. So what? That meant *nothing*.

Yet for the first time since all the moving around had begun, Aaron actually felt as though there was someplace he wanted to be. Someone he wanted to be with. A laugh he wanted to hear again.

"Forget the Smackdown," he whispered. He drew a sharp breath and headed for Claire.

The hall was filling with fellow students, and one after another slid in front of him. He darted between them as if he were wearing his blades.

Suddenly the door to the nurse's office swung open, and J.D. Harms stepped out.

Aaron gasped as J.D. turned his way and read Aaron's shirt.

"Don't agree with your theory on procrastination," J.D. said. Then he reached for Aaron's neck. "*Never* put off until tomorrow what you can put off forever."

"Can't say I agree with that!" said Aaron, pulling back just out of J.D.'s grasp.

Aaron didn't want to fight. On the other hand, there was something about this guy that really got to him. His smug attitude. His superiority. It was as if he were saying, *I'm the baddest of the bad. I can do anything I want, and there's nothing you can do or say that can stop me.*

Actually, there were about a half dozen things Aaron could think of right off to stop this guy. He was big and lumbering and slow. Aaron was lean and fast. And his dad had made sure he knew how to take care of himself.

Aaron looked past J.D. and saw Claire staring at him, eyes wide. He thought about what Bertram had said. He knew that fighting wouldn't be the smartest choice. But his only other option was running away, and how would *that* make him look to Claire?

He was trapped.

And to make matters worse, students started clustering around them. "Fight, fight, fight!" they began to chant.

At that moment a miracle happened. Something even better than the story Bertram had made up about eighth-graders being zapped back in time and away from their troubles.

Two young women appeared and led Claire away. Then the crowd closed in, ensuring that even if Claire looked back, she wouldn't be able to see a thing.

"How fast can you run?" Aaron asked.

J.D.'s forehead crinkled. He lunged—and Aaron turned and ran, laughing and hollering.

He bobbed and weaved through the disappointed crowd, leaping over at least two legs set out to trip him. He heard J.D.'s crashing footfalls behind him—and suddenly realized he only barely knew the layout of this place.

"Hey, no running in the hall!" a teacher shouted.

Aaron ignored the words. From the sound of things, so did J.D.

Aaron heard the behemoth's labored breathing and a series of loud impacts that could only be J.D. punching lockers in frustration as he ran.

Aaron tried to think. He was heading *away* from all the administrative offices. That seemed to leave him two choices: He could duck into a classroom, or he could take the chase outside.

A classroom door appeared, and Aaron hauled it open. A messy science lab sprawled out before him, and a plan formed in his mind.

"Can we say *expelled*?" Aaron whispered.

He ran into the empty classroom. He turned in time to see J.D. stomp into the doorway behind him, slam the door shut, and lock it. Aaron hid behind a long black workstation while J.D.'s back was turned.

"Huh?" he heard J.D. say. "Come out, you wuss. Let's just get this over with. You know you got it comin'."

I was just thinking the same about you, Aaron thought.

"Listen, I've apologized," Aaron said. He held still as J.D. stalked near him. "I'll apologize again. I wasn't looking where I was going. I was out of it, and I'm sorry. Let's just forget it before things get out of hand."

J.D. stopped. "You want to just forget about it?"

An image popped into Aaron's mind. He pictured himself standing in front of a possessed Mack truck, a huge, out-of-control machine. Something that didn't speak his language and wouldn't bother listening even if it could.

I'm a truck, it would say. *You're not. I'm going to run you down. Duh. What is there to talk about?*

"You are *so* dead," J.D. said as he reached for Aaron.

With a sigh, Aaron leaped over a desk, knocking a handful of glass vials to the floor. Glass shattered, and he avoided the mess. J.D. followed him, crushing the glass beneath his feet.

Aaron positioned himself on one side of a workstation and waited. J.D. approached from the other and reached out again. Aaron stayed in place as long as he could, then darted back. J.D. fell across the workstation, sending two racks of test tubes and a microscope to the floor.

Aaron leaped over another workstation, again careful to avoid the mess. His feet swept out and kicked more expensive equipment to the ground. Then he hit the floor running, his shoes never going near the chemicals he'd spilled or the glass he'd broken.

J.D. raced after him, throwing stools, shattering glass, breaking one thing after another.

"Stay in one *place*!" J.D. hollered.

Yeah, right! Aaron thought.

A sudden pounding came from the classroom door, followed by the rattle of the knob and a jingle of keys.

"Somebody help!" Aaron shouted. "He's going crazy!"

J.D. roared as he lunged for Aaron, breaking even more school property without coming within a foot of his prey.

"Come on, man, it can't be that bad!" Aaron yelled as loudly as he could. "This is a good school!"

J.D. hesitated, another stool held high over his head. "What?"

The door opened, and three teachers piled in. One of them was tall and muscular like a football coach. He had short-cropped brown hair and looked as though he spent almost all of his time outside.

"Put it down, Harms!" the coach said. He set his meaty arms on his hips.

J.D. turned, frowned, and set the stool on the floor.

"Look at this place!" another teacher exclaimed. He had graying hair and a goatee.

The last teacher was younger than the other two, with thinning blond hair, glasses, and a tie with no jacket.

Aaron watched as J.D. surveyed all the damage. The guy appeared to be snapping out of a trance. He frowned at the glass fragments attached to his boots and all the chemicals spilled over his jacket, shirt, and shoes.

Then he looked at Aaron. No stains. No glass. Nothing.

"Hey, waitaminute," J.D. began.

"J.D., I'm just saying it can't be that bad!" Aaron cried with as much fake sincerity as he could manage. "School's not easy for anyone, but you don't have to do this!"

The coach shook his head. "I should have known something like this was bound to happen."

J.D.'s face dropped as he seemed to realize the trouble he was in. He pointed at Aaron. "It's *his* fault!"

"Oh, I'm sure he twisted your arm to bust up the place," the coach said. Then he turned to Aaron. "Son, are you all right?"

Aaron let out a shuddering breath, then put a hand to his head theatrically. "I think so. He just went crazy. I tried talking to him—"

J.D. whirled on Aaron. "You set me up!"

This time when J.D. lunged, Aaron stayed where he was. J.D.'s heavy bulk smashed into him, carrying them both to the floor.

"Ow!" Aaron yelped. He saw J.D.'s arm up, his hand balled into a fist. Then the coach was on J.D., dragging him away.

"I don't care who your father knows," the coach said to J.D. "You're out of here!"

J.D. looked back to Aaron. "You must think you're pretty smart. You're not. We're gonna settle this. Maybe not here and now, but the time and place are *gonna* come. You know they are."

Aaron had a feeling J.D. was right, and it made his stomach sink.

"Yeah, J.D.," the coach said. "You keep blaming everyone else for your problems. Just see where that gets you in the real world."

J.D. shrugged off the coach's restraining hands. "I know more about the real world than any of you. Believe it."

Aaron now wondered if he had made a terrible mistake. He really hadn't been thinking about the future. In fact, he rarely did. That was something he and his mom always used to talk about, back in the days when they talked in more than just his dreams.

But what was he supposed to have done? Let J.D. put him in the hospital?

A sudden rumble of thunder sounded, even though blinding sunlight poured through the windows. The teachers looked at each other.

"It couldn't be," the coach said.

The other two teachers glanced around nervously as the thunder came again and the air seemed to crackle with energy. They stepped away from Aaron and J.D. and looked toward a collection of students gathered in the hall near the open door.

"Run!" yelled the teacher with the goatee. "It's happening again. *Run!*"

Aaron didn't know *what* was happening. It was

almost as if he could feel J.D.'s rage gathering around them like an electrical storm.

Suddenly a deafening thunderclap sounded in the science lab and a hissing blue-white streak of lightning rose from the floor. It wavered for a moment like a snake, then shot out and encircled Aaron and J.D.

Aaron felt a shocking surge of energy move through him. He shuddered and saw J.D.'s wildly grinning face.

"It's true," J.D. said. "The stories. The M.I.N.D. Machine. The past. All *true!*"

Aaron had no idea what was happening or what J.D. was talking about. He just wanted to be somewhere else. Anywhere else.

He gasped as he felt a part of himself being lifted out of his body. Below him was the classroom he'd been standing in. Then he was floating into the chaos of Wetherford's hallways.

Creatures were roaming through the school, students fleeing them in terror. Aaron blinked and realized that the creatures were *dinosaurs*—all kinds of dinosaurs! Somehow he knew that they were Wetherford students, too.

Whoa.

A boy burst through the gym doors and flew down the corridor. He ducked into a classroom, where three raptors cornered him.

"That's the one," the closest raptor said as he leaped onto a nearby desk and glared at the boy. "The only one who can stop it."

Aaron saw the guy grab a heavy globe from the teacher's desk and run for the huge windows. He hurled the globe at one of the windows to break it, then leaped through the open space.

At that moment Aaron's vision blurred. He heard roars of giant beasts. The crashing of waves. A raging wind. J.D.'s hearty laughter. Then he was spinning until all his senses deserted him.

He *still* wanted to be somewhere else. Anywhere else.

Suddenly he *was*.

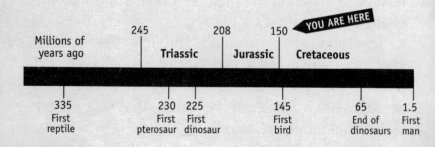

PART ONE

BRONTO-A-GO-GO

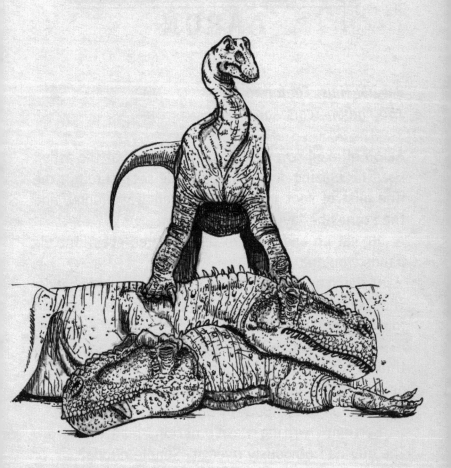

CHAPTER 1

AARON

Beverly Hills, California
150 Million Years Ago

Aaron blinked several times as he stared at the ashen sky. The blazing sun strained to be seen through the fine mist of soot in the air. The air was muggy, and the stones he lay upon were warm.

He sat up and tried to rub his tired eyes. But his hands wouldn't reach!

Drawing a sharp breath, Aaron examined his hands. They were purple and yellow, and scaly. They ended in four fingers, three of which sported sharp claws.

He looked down his body and saw fat, scaly thighs. A tail slapped around behind him. *His* tail. A pair of crests on his forehead wiggled.

I'm a dinosaur. Back in time.

Bertram's writing wasn't fiction, realized Aaron. The guy had obviously lived it. Simple enough.

Aaron passed out.

* * *

Aaron woke. He blinked several times at the grayish sky. *Take two.* He shuddered.

"Okay," he said, feeling his razor-lined maw open and close, his tongue wriggle around. A few bugs flew by, one of them sailing into his mouth. He sat up again, tried to spit it out, and swallowed by accident.

"Ack!" he yelled. Then he rose on shaky legs and looked around.

Aaron was standing on a wide shelf of rock carved into the side of a mountain. Similar shelves lined the way down into a lush, green, mist-blanketed valley. Many of the shelves were broken into columns.

"This is not for me," Aaron said. "Sorry. No."

When he spoke, he heard his own human voice in his head, but from his dinosaur mouth came a weird clucking sound, along with several high squeals.

Some instinct told him that he wasn't *really* talking at all. The animal noises he heard were coming from him. His voice was registering only in his mind.

Then another sound came: *Crrrrrawwwwwwwwww!*

He whirled and saw the weirdest-looking bird he'd ever encountered staring at him from a high ledge. It was about the size of Cory the Compsognathus, and its wildly colored array of feathers gave it the appearance of a peacock mixed with a turkey. Bright sky-blue feathers, striking golden feathers, and bold crimson feathers were all mixed with softer pastel shades.

"Hey, Birdie, what's up?" Aaron asked.

Birdie swayed the huge feather duster of a tail it carried behind itself and fluttered its wings. It snapped its beak defensively.

Snap-snap!

"Listen, you wouldn't happen to know where they stuck the exit door, would ya?" Aaron asked. He understood, of course, that he was speaking to a bird, but on the other hand, he was a dinosaur, so that made it okay.

Birdie spat at him.

"Hey!" Aaron yelled. "Now that was just *rude*."

Birdie hissed, turned its back, raised its tail feathers, and let out a little *pffft*.

The smell was awful. Aaron waved his claws in the air.

"Excuse me," he said. "You know, if I end up having to stay here, I'm definitely going to have to find things to eat, and you're not exactly making it hard for me to picture you roasting over an open fire!"

Birdie turned around, lowered its head, and cooed. Aaron's shoulders slumped. He suddenly felt like a jerk. Okay, it didn't seem likely that a little spittle and a fart were meant to be a friendly greeting, but what did *he* know about these animals?

"It's okay," Aaron said. He looked around and saw a couple of rust-colored pillars nearby. Slowly he climbed onto one of them.

Birdie drew back a few feet.

"It's okay," Aaron said. "It's cool. I'm not gonna eat ya. I promise."

All he really wanted to do was calm the poor thing down.

As he climbed from one pillar to another, each a little higher than the one before, he gazed into the soulful eyes of the birdlike dinosaur. Birdie didn't seem to have any pals around, and Aaron could identify with feeling scared and alone. Everywhere he went, he was the new kid.

Actually, thinking about what had just happened to him in those terms made it a whole lot less scary.

"Listen, we can be buds," Aaron said. "You can show me around, and I'll help keep you safe."

Birdie held its ground as Aaron stepped onto the little dinosaur's ledge.

"This is something," Aaron said. "Terrace apartments. Nice view. Reminds me of when we were stationed in Hawaii."

Birdie craned its neck and rustled its feathers.

Aaron grunted as he climbed the pillars. He felt so strange in this new body. His legs were bent back at a funny angle, and he walked hunched over, a little like the way he moved when he was blading. His neck was about twice the length that it should have been, and his arms were really tiny. And if that weren't bad enough, the weight of his tail kept threatening to throw off his balance.

Still, he was able to adjust to his new form a little more with every step.

"You know what the strangest thing is?" he asked Birdie. "No, wait. I should never say that. It can *always* get stranger."

He took a few steps toward the birdlike dinosaur, who squawked and hopped in place excitedly.

"The strangest—well, *one* of the strangest things is that I'm really not feeling all that bad over this," Aaron said. "I mean, there's got to be advantages to being a dinosaur, right? No classes. No Ms. Attila the Hun. You can sleep as late as you want. Do whatever you please. I'll miss my dad. I mean, that sucks. Colonel Charmin's pretty straight up. And no pizza, no DVDs, no Pamela Anderson Lee—" He sighed. "And no Claire. Maybe this isn't such a good thing after all." Aaron leaned forward, his hand outstretched to pet Birdie's flank.

Suddenly Birdie went ballistic!

With wings spread wide, Birdie leaped high. Claws extended from the edges of Birdie's wings—*Where did those come from?*—and one raked across Aaron's face.

He felt a searing pain and stumbled back, nearly top-pling from the ledge.

Then he righted himself and looked at the raised tail feathers of the birdlike dinosaur as the animal trotted off.

"You little turkey!" Aaron hollered. "Oh, man, that's it. First J.D., now this? No way!"

Aaron ran after the little dinosaur. Birdie leaped and fluttered its wings, but it didn't go airborne. Its arms looked like they were missing the muscles birds used to take flight.

"You hold still!" Aaron called. "We are going to have a serious talk!"

Birdie made another little *pffft* and leaped to a higher column. Aaron chased the little dinosaur, rising higher and higher as he jumped from one terrace to another, zigzagging up the side of the mountain.

The mist thickened, and the heat Aaron had felt earlier lessened. Aaron lunged at Birdie twice, missing the little dinosaur both times. Soon he was laughing, enjoying the chase. His anger also cooled.

This was just a fun game. He wasn't going to eat Birdie; they were just playing tag, that's all.

"I'm gonna getcha," Aaron called, just as if he were chasing after one of the neighbor's children the way he'd done when they lived in Virginia. "I'm gonna *getcha!*"

He also liked that the chase gave him something to think about other than how he had gotten here and what he was going to do now that he had arrived. Just ahead, Birdie chirped and cawed, its wings flapping like some exotic fan.

They made it up three more levels. Then three more. Aaron smelled something foul from on high and craned his neck. The heat from the ground returned, even as the mist grew thicker and colder around him.

"Gonna getcha!" Aaron called. He leaped onto another column, then an even higher one, and jumped onto a long, flat stretch.

Aaron hesitated as he saw Birdie racing ahead, the mist swallowing up the birdlike dinosaur. They had reached some kind of flat area. Maybe they were on the top of the mountain, on some wide plateau. The mist made it hard to tell anything for sure.

The rock beneath his feet was slippery and uneven. He walked deeper into the mist, a dull red glow rising from just ahead.

Crrrrrawwwwwwwwww!

The odd mix of cool and warm air buffeted him as he took several more steps and saw Birdie racing toward a small rise. The tiny dinosaur leaped onto the rise, then flung itself forward, dipping low and out of view, then rising, its wings flapping hard. Aaron watched as Birdie circled overhead, gave one last tiny *pffft,* and sailed off.

Cautiously Aaron approached the rise. He poked his head beyond the little border and trembled at what lay deep below: a swirling mass of molten lava!

"This is a volcano," he whispered. "Dinosaurs. Volcanoes. Right..."

He took a better look around and saw little cracks in the earth, venting steam. He slowly backed up.

The mist enshrouded the lip of the volcano, leaving only a dim crimson glow. Aaron kept stepping back gingerly, expecting the ground beneath him to collapse.

"You're gonna fall," someone said.

Aaron spun, his tail whacking a small rock from the ground. He saw another figure duck to avoid the stone. A dinosaur like him.

"Watch out!" the other dinosaur called.

Aaron stood still. "Sorry." He looked over and saw that he'd been so scared he'd almost stepped right off the plateau into nothingness.

"How are you doing?" the other dinosaur asked. "Are you all right?"

Aaron nodded. He studied the dinosaur before him. Two crests on the skull. Tiny arms. Powerful legs. The teeth in his snout were long and slender, but those in his cheeks looked like knife blades. His body was gray with amber streaks. His crests were crimson, yellow, and violet.

Aaron pointed feebly at his companion and heard some of the dumbest words he'd ever spoken dribbling from his lips. "You're a dinosaur. This is a volcano."

"Yeah," the other dino said. "Um, are you still at the 'fire bad, tree pretty' stage, or can we have a conversation?"

Aaron thought he recognized the voice. "Bertram?"

The dinosaur nodded. "I bet you're wishing you had gone to the nurse's office a little sooner, huh?"

For some reason, Aaron felt annoyed by the statement. He'd made a choice. He could live with it.

Then he realized he was being overwhelmed with a lot of strange feelings toward Bertram. Envy, rivalry, resentment—and a bond that felt unbreakable.

What was happening to him?

"You've been through this before," Aaron said anxiously. "You know what to do, right?"

Bertram looked away. "This isn't like the other time. Everything's different."

"Um, well, what are we?"

"We're predators," Bertram said. "Dilophosaurus."

"No, I mean..." Aaron struggled for the words. "Why do I feel like I just want to strangle you? We barely know each other!"

"Oh. *That.*" Bertram shrugged. "Well, beyond being trapped here with no way back, beyond having to deal with a whole ton of active volcanoes that might blow at any second, and beyond the fact that one person I *know* you're not going to want to deal with is here, it gets worse."

"How's that?" Aaron asked in a small voice.

Bertram put his claw on Aaron's shoulder. "We're brothers. Or rather, these dinosaurs we're inhabiting are brothers."

Aaron reeled at the thought, just as the sound of low, throaty laughter rose from somewhere in the valley deep below.

CHAPTER 2

J.D.

"I love it!" J.D. hollered. He whooped and laughed, leaping around in his new dinosaur body. "This is perfect! Perfect!"

He laughed until he nearly fell on his side.

J.D. felt pumped and primed. He trembled with excitement and sheer raw power. He was a dinosaur.

A dinosaur!

All his life he had dreamed of something like this happening to him. He was free of the life into which he'd been born, free to make his own rules, free to decide his own future.

He could go where he wanted. Do what he wanted. No one could stop him. And if they were dumb enough to try, then J.D. "Judgment Day" Harms would show them *exactly* how he had earned his nickname at Wetherford Junior High.

He looked around the green valley. There were other dinosaurs nearby. He could smell them.

And he was *hungry*.

Laughing, J.D. leaped around some more. He almost fell over, but he stopped himself, realizing he might not know how to get up again.

His body was unbelievably powerful. The earth shook when he leaped!

Low roars came from the distance, and J.D. followed the sounds. The stomping of his heavy feet made the ground tremble, and he felt a little wobbly, but he guessed that was normal. It wasn't every day a person got tossed back in time and into the body of a dinosaur.

He mashed the earth as he went along. He growled and spat. This place was great!

His neck bobbed and his tail swished. That was a little weird. And for some reason he couldn't quite focus his vision. He saw slightly different images out of each eye, and everything looked flat, like a TV show.

Whatever. He'd get the hang of things soon enough.

He climbed a small rise and saw a dinosaur lapping water from a huge puddle. The dinosaur was gray with orange splotches, and it looked like a T. rex, only bigger, with jaws that reminded J.D. of a pair of scissors.

The dinosaur's head swiveled, and muddy water splashed as it rose to fix J.D. with its dark eyes.

J.D. laughed. "Hey, Ugly, what are you lookin' at?"

Ugly was looking at *him*. Drool dripped from Ugly's maw. The gray and orange dinosaur sprinted up the rise and stopped just before J.D., studying him. Ugly's breath was rank.

J.D.'s heart skipped a beat as Ugly moved in closer. He hadn't expected Ugly to move so fast. Or to be so *big*.

J.D. blinked, trying to make sense out of what he was seeing. In his time, *he* was the baddest of the bad. The biggest thing out there. The tyrant king. It only made sense that he was the same in the age of dinosaurs.

Yet Ugly looked at least three times his size!

What was going on here? Was he in the body of some defenseless youth? Not a full-grown dinosaur?

Ugly opened its jaws, raised its tiny front claws, and roared.

J.D. sensed it was a challenge. One this predator might have issued to another of its kind.

All things considered, though, it was really more of a joke.

Ugly was *laughing* at him.

J.D. launched himself at the bigger dinosaur. Ugly yelped in surprise as J.D.'s round hoofs hit him hard in the belly. Suddenly they were tumbling down the other side of the hill, rolling and bouncing. Ugly's head hit a huge, shattered tree trunk, and he lay on the ground panting as J.D. floundered to a stop before him.

"You want a fight?" J.D. asked, getting up slowly. "You came to the right guy." He glared at the dazed predator. "I may be little. But one thing I've *never* been is defenseless."

Sounds came from the hill. J.D. turned, expecting to see two more big dinosaurs like Ugly. Instead, the dinosaurs moving down the hill behind him were big, fat-bellied plodders with large plates sticking up on their backs and spikes at the ends of their tails.

"What are you lookin' at?" J.D. asked.

He heard Ugly moving behind him, so he stomped the other dinosaur again without even looking its way. Ugly groaned and settled down.

The first of the spike-tails came closer. It had ugly brown and red splotches that looked like a rash all over its scaly hide.

"Just move away from it slowly," Splotchy said. "We'll take it from here."

J.D. frowned inwardly. What were these lame-os talking about?

Suddenly the dinosaur behind J.D. rose and roared. J.D. jumped. He couldn't help himself. The sound was like a siren going off in his ear. He refused to turn and look at the predator again. He knew enough not to encourage guys like this.

The other leaf-eating dinosaur ambled up beside

its friend, the earth trembling with its footsteps. It had dull yellow stripes across its blubbery brown girth.

"Really," Splotchy said. "Move. *Now*."

J.D. laughed. *Yeah, right*. He was going to take orders from this pair of wusses. "Is there some reason I should?"

The spike-tails were silent.

"Ah, get out of here before I eat both of you!" J.D. said.

The dinosaur with the rash turned to its buddy. "He doesn't get it."

J.D. felt the breath of the predator upon his neck. Okay, Ugly wasn't going away. J.D. looked at its face—and froze.

Ugly leaned in closer, and J.D. saw his own reflection in Ugly's dark eyes.

J.D. had a little head with baby teeth. A neck that had to go back a half dozen feet. A body that was round and tubby. A tail ending in an itsy-bitsy little point.

He was a long-neck. A plant-eater!

And Ugly looked as though it wanted to eat *him*.

J.D. backed away on wobbly tree-trunk-sized legs.

"Now there's something I never thought I'd see," Splotchy said.

"I dunno," the other spike-tail added. "I kinda wanted to see him get eaten."

"Well, we *can't*. Come on."

J.D. saw the veggiesaurs come around him. A different dinosaur appeared in each of his wall eyes—Splotchy on his left side, and the striped one on his right.

He angled his head a little, so that he could see what was right in front of him, and was surprised to see Ugly backing away. The plant-eaters stalked the predator. They were just as big as Ugly, and *they* had thick tails bearing three-foot or four-foot spikes.

Ugly stopped near a couple of sixty-five-foot-tall pine trees and chomped at the air. J.D. figured the predator was trying to scare off the spike-tails. It wasn't working.

Splotchy pivoted on one hip, spinning its entire body in a blur. Its tail shot around and smashed one of the trees next to Ugly into splinters.

Ugly grunted and jumped back.

Splotchy's pal surged in and turned another tree to toothpicks.

Ugly spun and got out of there. He didn't exactly run. It was more of a trot.

Choice, man...

J.D. had figured the day would come when he might be in that position, too. He might have been the biggest and toughest guy in the eighth grade, but graduation was coming up—and high school. What was he going to do then?

That was one reason he had been so blasted happy that Bertram's stories had turned out to be true.

Another was that he never again had to face what waited for him at home.

"So, J.D., you okay?" Splotchy asked.

J.D. turned. He raised his snout. "Sure."

Splotchy's buddy laughed. "It's just with you shaking like a little kid and everything, we got kinda worried."

J.D.'s entire body tensed. Another challenge. Perfect.

"Hey, J.D.," Splotchy said, "I bet you don't even remember us."

The spike-tails started to circle him.

Splotchy's friend chortled. "This is classic. I never thought I'd see the day when J.D. Harms was scared of us."

"You still haven't," J.D. said. He heard the tremble in his own voice.

The spike-tails started beating their tails on the earth. He stood his ground as they got closer—and got bigger. At least that was how it looked.

Suddenly he couldn't even see them. What was going on here?

Krrrrrackkkkkkkk!

J.D. reeled as his head snapped back on its long neck, and he slipped into a puddle the size of a small lake. Mud and muck flew everywhere as he landed.

"Ugh!" he groaned, his head throbbing. He rolled around in the mud while the spike-tails laughed, their bellies jiggling.

J.D. blinked a couple of times—and understood.

He had no depth perception. That was why he thought the spike-tails were so small and he was so big. He thought they were closer to him—but they weren't.

His eyes were on either side of his head. He couldn't even see what was right in front of him because of that.

On top of that, his neck ached in a dozen different places.

J.D. kept scrambling until he managed to position his feet just right and was able to stand up. He looked down his long neck and at his flank to finally accept the truth.

He was a lousy leaf-muncher. Just like the spike-tailed dweebs.

How lame was *that*?

J.D. had been certain that he was some amazing predator, and he hadn't really thought about how he'd been standing on all fours or how weird and flat the world looked. All he'd cared about was that he was out of Wetherford and that the dreams he'd been having ever since the "electrical accident"

at school seemed to be coming true.

He was in a different place, a different time, and here he could do what he wanted, when he wanted, with no one giving him problems. Not his teachers, not his parents, not the other students. He was finally in control.

J.D. looked over at the circling spike-tails.

They were bigger than he had realized. Each of them was probably twice his size. And there was something inside him that felt scared every time one of them scraped its tail along the ground.

Come on, we're all plant-eaters; we can talk about this...

"Shut up," J.D. muttered.

The spike-tails froze.

"Pardon?" Splotchy said.

"Wasn't talking to you," J.D. said. He lowered his head just a little.

The plant-eaters laughed again.

J.D. wasn't going to put up with this. He'd been able to defend himself all his life. Who cared what body he was in?

"I'm givin' you guys one chance to back down," J.D. said. "I don't know what kind of history we got. I don't know who either of you is. Clean slate, got it?"

"Nope," Splotchy said. "We're just not that smart." The dinosaur slammed its spiked tail on the ground again.

"Come on," J.D. said. His tone was as light as he could manage. "We're all plant-eaters. So I know you're not gonna eat me. What else can you do to me?"

Splotchy laughed as he advanced on J.D. "Come on, Fred. Let's show him."

CHAPTER 3

CLAIRE

Claire woke feeling groggy and in a bad mood, as she did whenever she overslept. Her teeth were bothering her, as if she had been grinding them half the night, and she had a headache. She rolled over in bed and growled when her head hit a rock.

A *rock*?

Why was a rock in her bed? And what was she doing *growling*?

She yawned and tried to settle back to sleep. Forget the rock, forget the growl, forget all of it. She was tired, she felt like garbage, and she needed a sick day, that was all.

Weird sounds came from all around. The buzzing of insects. The lapping of waves. The distant caw of a bird.

"Must have left the TV on," she muttered.

Someone nudged her.

"Come on, Ma," she whispered. "Can't you see I'm sick? You wouldn't want me to have bags under my eyes or something. Have to buy extra makeup. Not like you don't make me wear enough. Gotta be ready for those big auditions. I *like* flying out to L.A. three times a month. It's not like I should have any control over my own life. Now *lemme sleep*!"

The nudge came again, followed by a small yip—then a bite.

Claire whirled, her arms, legs, and tail tensing.

Tail!

Claire opened her eyes wide and took in the sight of two dozen little beak-faced reptiles gazing down at her.

She shuddered.

This wasn't her four-poster bed, and there were no sheer white curtains, no pictures of the sea, no crystal butterfly collection. Instead, she was on a rocky shore with a gaggle of strange creatures peering curiously at her.

Two of the reptiles hissed and moved in for another little bite—

"Get off me!" Claire cried. Inside her mind her words sounded like human words, but the racket that came out of her mouth wasn't anything remotely human. It was a roar. An *animal* roar.

The tiny chicklike reptiles moved in a blur, running in crazy curving patterns all along the beach. Claire watched them go, picturing extras and crew members on a set scrambling to obey the booming commands of a director.

This isn't real. It can't be, she thought.

But her instincts told her it was.

A good actor lives and dies by instinct, by living the moment, by believing, her agent, Laura, often told her. Her parents echoed these ideas.

Claire was a good actor, and she knew the advice rising in her thoughts was correct.

Although she'd rather be out in her backyard studying bugs. She *loved* bugs. Bugs, snakes, spiders, all that stuff. Couldn't get enough.

If not for the Internet, she'd never be able to see those things up close at all. And if not for Bertram Phillips showing her how to create security lockouts and double blinds on her PC so that her parents didn't know what she was up to, she never would.

"Okay," she whispered. "You know what you're seeing is real. So *believe*."

She took a good look at her surroundings.

The sea was before her. The sky was ashen except for the shafts of bright sunlight straining to penetrate the bits of gray and black drifting overhead. Behind her lay a lush forest with strange, exotic trees that seemed impossibly tall. Beyond the trees a long row of mountain crests poked the clouds.

Okay, I'm in Hawaii or something. Only the mountains are taller. A lot taller. And I have a TAIL.

She tried to stand up, but her body wasn't responding the way she'd expected. She felt a surge of panic coming on. Then she thought about what the other students at Wetherford Junior High called her.

Crystal Claire. Don't drop her or she'll break!

She *hated* that. She had always hated being treated as if she were some fragile, delicate thing.

Sure, those were the parts she always ended up with in the Wetherford Players productions, but she was acting! That wasn't her. Why did everyone have to treat her as though she were such a wuss?

And why did she put up with it?

Right, like nothing bad's ever happened to me. Just try going on a cattle call with two thousand other thirteen-year-olds and being told "You're too short," "You're too tall," "You're too fair," "You're too small," "We wanted someone sunnier," "We were thinking a little more dark," "We just don't see it in your eyes," "Sorry, you've got to really want this, you know."

Or having to look at her mom and dad every time she failed. Those thin smiles. The comforting arm that was stiff with frustration, the reassuring touch tense with disappointment.

You've got a gift and you should use it, her agent whispered in her mind. *Do you know how few people your age can even get an agent? Especially without living in L.A.?*

So far, despite all her hard work, only her hands

and the back of her head had made it onto the big screen. But she was tough. She'd keep going.

You just have to want it.

Claire was no longer sure she wanted an acting career. But looking out at this place, she thought of something she *did* want.

The world as she knew it had changed. And she was going to deal with it. From this moment on, she was going to be a warrior princess, not a crystal princess. If there was any rescuing to be done, she would be the one to do it. Simple as that.

First things first, Claire told herself. *To know your character, you have to know yourself.*

After figuring out a way of flopping onto her belly, she used her little hands to get herself to a sitting position. Then she walked to the shore and peered at her reflection in the water.

She was a dinosaur.

Okay.

She turned her face from side to side. Jaws like a pair of scissors. Tiny hands with sharp claws. Kinda like a rex, only meaner and weirder-looking. Her scales were metallic gray with thin rust-colored stripes. She looked like the Terminator of dinosaurs.

Wicked.

Her belly rumbled.

Oh, right. Dinos are always hungry.

She spotted a long silver fish swimming near the

shore. Darting forward, she snatched it up in her maw, bit it in half, chewed for a while, spit out the bones, and took a big swallow.

Yum!

This was like having her own sushi bar or something. Oh, sure, what she had just done was disgusting, no question. But it was right in character.

Cool.

Claire didn't mind performing under these circumstances. She always pictured herself as her character, so seeing herself in the body of some gigantic predator and acting tough pretty much went together for her. But there was one thing missing.

An audience.

Claire walked down the shore, hoping to spot someone else. She saw no one, but her nose caught a scent.

Fresh meat. Good to eat!

Whoa. It seemed there were some instincts she would have to rein in.

Claire found an opening between the wall of tall trees behind the shore and climbed several rises. The smell was richer now. Juicier.

It was the smell of *fear*.

That stopped her. She cautiously approached the base of another low hill, crouching to make sure she wouldn't be seen by anyone on the other side. The sounds of grunting drifted toward her dino ears, but in her mind, she heard the English language.

"I'm telling you, Melissa, I've got it all under control."

The mind-voice belonged to a guy, and it seemed awfully familiar to Claire.

"This is crazy! It can't be happening!"

Claire didn't recognize the second mind-voice at all. She could easily make out that it was a young woman, but nothing more. The fear Claire was picking up came from both of them.

"Something's coming!" the young woman with the high voice squealed. "I can feel it!"

"You're safe," the guy said. "You're with me."

Anger rose in Claire. She had heard those words before, and from the same infuriating jerk.

It was Reggie Firth. Red hair. Freckles. Mr. Macho. The great protector.

Sheesh.

Claire trudged up the hill. If there was something after these two, maybe the sight of her would drive it away. In fact, she hoped that was exactly what would happen. Her footfalls sounded like thunder. *Good!*

Claire reached the top of the hill and looked down on two tiny dinosaurs—they looked tiny to her, anyway. She really hadn't been able to get any sense of scale yet, just a sense that she was really, *really* big.

You're gonna make it big, Claire! You know we wouldn't say that if we didn't believe it!

Mom and Dad had been right. If only they could see her now. A little laugh escaped her. It sounded more like a rumble and made the dinosaurs below quiver.

One of them had a dome-shaped head with a ridge running around it to his wide eyes. He stood upright, his tail whipping from side to side. And he was pink.

A hardhead? *Had* to be Reggie.

The other dinosaur stood on her rear two legs, which were thick and sported the biggest clawed feet Claire had ever seen. Her belly was huge and bloated, her arms flabby and ending in hands topped with spikelike claws. Her neck looked like a beanstalk and was just as long as her torso. Her head was small, and her jaws were open wide as she sputtered and spat in terror. She was crimson with black spots, like a ladybug.

Claire looked around, trying to find the threat. She didn't see anything. She didn't smell anything.

"It's gonna eat us!" the young woman hollered, her claws waving in Claire's direction.

Oh, wow, thought Claire, *they're afraid of ME!*

Well, all she had to do was open her mouth and tell them who she was, and they'd stop being afraid in a hurry, no matter what she looked like. She was about to do that when Reggie stepped in front of his companion, the mini long-neck.

"You—You j-j-just stay behind me," Reggie sputtered. "I'll handle this thing!"

Claire chortled. She couldn't help herself. Reggie was about a quarter of her size. She could bounce him around like a basketball. What a macho dummy!

She couldn't help it. She started laughing. But the sound of her laughter was drowned out by the roars coming from her dinosaur body.

Reggie trembled—and ran!

Claire's eyes widened. The guy had abandoned his new princess! What a wimp! What a weenie!

And all because of *her*. Oh, this was too good!

The young woman in the body of the compact long-neck looked frozen with fear. Claire got her laughter under control and took a deep breath.

"Don't you just hate guys like that?" Claire asked.

The ladybug-colored long-neck stopped shaking. Her slack mouth closed. She looked around nervously, then nodded.

"Yeah," she said. "I really do."

Claire tromped down the hill. The other dinosaur held her ground.

"I'm Melissa," the mini long-neck said.

"Cool," Claire said. She was about to introduce herself when other sounds and smells drifted her way. She saw another huge predator like herself angrily burst through a clearing a mile off, glance at her, shrug, and move off in the other direction.

Whoa, she thought. *So that's how the others see me.*

Pretty scary.

Claire listened more closely to the sounds. It was a chant of some kind, and it sounded like, "Fight! Fight! Fight!"

"You know," Claire said to the mini long-neck, "I'm not a hundred percent sure we made it out of junior high at all. What about you?"

Melissa shook her head.

They followed the sounds and crested another rise. Down in the valley, another small long-neck was getting pummeled by a pair of spike-tails.

"I'm sayin' this for the last time!" the long-neck cried. "I don't know what kind of history we got; I don't know who either of you is. Clean slate if you back off right now, got it?"

The spike-tails weren't listening—but Claire was.

A clean slate.

That gave Claire an idea. No one knew who she was back here. She could be anyone, even the toughest girl in the eighth grade.

Now who would that be?

A week ago, Claire would have said Patience McCray, star of the Wetherford girls' basketball team. But Patience had been different lately.

Then there was Holly Cronk. No one knew much about her. She hardly ever spoke. She just glared at people—and sometimes jammed them into lockers if they were dumb enough to try to strike up a conversation with her.

"I didn't tell you what my name is," Claire said to Melissa. She turned, striking as dramatic a pose as she could and making sure to use the memory of Holly's voice to mask her own. "The name's Holly. Holly Cronk."

Melissa's eyes widened once more. Claire congratulated herself on an excellent choice and some authentic acting ability—even if it was from inside a dinosaur—then turned once more to look down at the fight. But she spun so quickly she tripped over her own feet and went tumbling down the mountainside, screaming and cursing—and heading right for the guys who were fighting!

CHAPTER 4

BERTRAM

Bertram and Aaron reached the base of the volcano and sat down to rest.

During the treacherous trip down the side of the volcano, they had paid little attention to anything but their footing on the narrow pathways. Neither of them had spoken more than a few words since Bertram had delivered the startling news that they were brothers.

Now Bertram wondered how Aaron felt about the revelation. He figured that it was news Aaron could have lived without.

"Being brothers complicates things," Bertram warned. "Our host bodies have a connection and a history we know nothing about. This could inform our decisions and our actions at critical times."

"Uh-huh," Aaron replied.

Bertram waited for Aaron to say something else. But apparently that was all Aaron had to say.

"You haven't read any of my stories, right?"

61

Bertram asked.

Aaron shook his head.

Bertram studied his companion. Aaron's vacant expression was already starting to get on Bertram's nerves.

"But you get the basic idea, don't you?" Bertram continued. "They're not stories at all. The M.I.N.D. Machine is real. It takes people out of their bodies and sends them to other times and places. I'm not sure exactly where we're at right now. Considering the volcanoes and everything, I'm guessing the California coast. But there are a lot of things that I've seen that aren't adding up, so I'm not exactly sure."

Aaron studied his claws a minute. "So you built the machine because you wanted to get away from it all? I guess I can understand that."

"I didn't do it consciously. The machine started out as my science fair project, and then something happened. It's hard to explain *exactly* what happened; I'm still trying to work it all out in my head. The bottom line is that I accidentally tapped into something. Time and space. The interconnectedness of all things. Matter not being created or destroyed, just changing form. Are you with me?"

Aaron nodded brightly. "No."

Bertram resisted the temptation to fly at his new brother and take a bite out of him. His maw trembled at the thought.

You've been through this before! Bertram told himself, willing the human part of him to stay in control. *These aren't your feelings. It's the predator mind.*

Aaron shrugged. "The machine got us here. Why can't it take us back?"

"Two problems with that," Bertram said. He stood and gestured for Aaron to come with him. His fellow Dilophosaurus sprang behind him, dual crests wiggling just a little.

The mist had lifted, and Bertram had no problem leading Aaron to the rocky incline where he had first found himself after the latest accident with the M.I.N.D. Machine.

The machine sat mashed into the ground, its shiny aluminum sides dented, its struts cracked, and all but two of its monitors shattered. Cables dangled from its ten-foot-long frame while bent or broken circuit boards drooped from its six-foot-high surface. A busted-up leather chair sat in its center, along with a keyboard dangling from one twisted arm.

"The first problem is that it's *here* when it should have stayed in our time," Bertram said. "The second is that it's busted, and there are no replacement parts back here and no power supply to tap into even if we could fix it."

"So things could be worse," Aaron said.

Bertram stared at him. "Is that supposed to be funny?"

"Huh?" Aaron asked. He looked at the machine as if he was transfixed. "No, it's just that you could weld some of those extra support beams that are falling off into a lightning rod to gather power, then dig around here for gold or other metals to make parts."

Bertram stared at him blankly. He was fully prepared to explain to Aaron how hopeless everything was and how Aaron's ideas made no sense at all—but he couldn't. Aaron was right.

"It just sounds to me like it's better to have the thing *here,* where you can do something with it, than somewhere else, where you can't even make it do anything," Aaron said. "And we've got time, right? It's not like there's any hurry or anything. We could take a month, and when we get back, it'll be like five seconds after we left or something."

Bertram blinked several times. He thought he was dreaming. Maybe there really *was* a lot more to Aaron than he'd thought. They might even be science buddies and be able to talk theory and break down the M.I.N.D. Machine's functions on a quantum level. "How'd you figure all this out?"

Aaron shrugged. "Watch a lot of movies, read a lot of comics, stuff just comes to you."

Straining to hide his disappointment, Bertram looked away. Sounds came from the distance.

"Oh, yeah. Another thing," Bertram said. "There are others like us. Lots of them this time. About two dozen, last time I looked."

"If there's a party, I'm not gonna be the one missin' it!" Aaron said. He sprinted away.

"Hold on!" Bertram called. It seemed that Bertram's earlier caution that there was someone here that Aaron might not want to run into had gone right past the guy. Bertram ran after Aaron, who was moving as if they hadn't just climbed down the side of a volcano at all.

Actually, Bertram's body *didn't* feel as tired and worn out as he thought it would. Or should.

He ran after Aaron, amazed at how easily Aaron had adapted to his new body and circumstances. Bertram relaxed and allowed himself to enjoy the sheer power and the amazing speed this new body allowed. It wasn't at all like being in the tanklike form of an Ankylosaurus.

They raced between trees, topped rises, and sped

across a narrow valley. Aaron stopped at the crest of another rise, and Bertram skidded to a halt beside him. He got there just in time to see an enormous predator slide down another rise and collide with a pair of Stegosaurus.

Bertram stared at the huge meat-eater. He had read about this predator, but it hadn't yet been named in his time. It was forty-five feet long, much bigger than a T. rex, and it looked meaner, too.

The scissor-jawed predator rose and growled at the two spike-tailed Stegosaurus. They beat their tails in return but backed away.

"He started it!" a splotchy Stegosaurus yelled, his voice nearly breaking.

"Yeah!" chorused his companion.

"I don't care who started it," the giant predator said. "I'm finishing it!"

Bertram looked at the dozen dinosaurs who had come running to see the fight. He counted a pair of Syntarsus, a Scutellosaurus, some scurrying Compsognathus, a duck-billed Maiasaura, a Pachy-cephalosaurus, a Heterodontosaurus, a Corythosaurus, a Diplodocus, and a Spinosaurus beyond the tiny brontosaur and the spike-tails. But that combination of dinosaurs just couldn't be! Not in one region and one period. Circling overhead, some colorfully feathered Archaeopteryx and bucket-mouthed pterosaurs squawked.

A Massospondylus came down from the ridge where the scissor-jaw had been standing. Its head bobbed on its long neck. "Guys, that's Holly! I'd listen if I were you!"

The crowd fell silent. The small Apatosaurus got to its feet while the spike-tails backed away. The brontosaurus looked unsteady from the walloping it had apparently taken, but it seemed determined to look as unaffected as possible.

"Hey!" the long-neck bronto yelled. "Do you know who I am?"

Scissor-jaw turned. "No idea."

"I'm J.D. Harms," the brontosaurus said. "And I don't need anyone fighting my battles for me. Understood?"

Bertram looked over to Aaron. The other Dilophosaurus's shoulders slumped.

"J.D.," Aaron said. "Just when I was thinkin' I could get to like it here."

Bertram watched sadly as the crowd below broke into bickering little groups. The scissor-jaw and J.D. started trading insults while the two spike-tailed Stegosaurus lumbered around as though they had just earned the bragging rights of a lifetime. Everyone in the valley looked miserable.

Bertram had kept his presence a secret from the others until now. He had wanted to learn as much as he could about their surroundings and to come up with some kind of plan.

He couldn't wait any longer. *Someone* had to get everyone calmed down and working together. He just wished it didn't have to be so hard. And he also wished it didn't have to be *him*.

Waving his hands, Bertram stepped down from the hill—and shuddered as a sudden and impossibly familiar wind kicked up around him.

"The M.I.N.D. Machine!" Bertram hollered.

Bertram's words quieted all the other lost students as blue-white lightning crackled around him and a booming voice exploded in his head.

He had a feeling the others could hear it, too.

"Bertram! Bertram, listen to me. This is Will Reilly. I don't know how long I've got, so I'm going to try to download what's happened into your head. If this works, you'll know everything I know!"

Bertram couldn't even *imagine* how this was possible. The machine was here. Smashed up. How could Will be using it to communicate with him from the future?

Then the lightning struck him, and a strange feeling came over Bertram. His mind was suddenly swimming in alien emotions and feelings.

He squeezed his eyes shut, and when he opened them again, he wasn't himself anymore.

CHAPTER 5

WILL

Will Reilly shuddered. He felt as if he'd been descending through impossibly deep waters, incredible pressures squeezing him from all sides. Now, suddenly, he was sitting still, on something solid.

From the corner of his eye, Will thought he saw crackling bursts of blue-white energy, like lightning. He turned his head, but they were gone, along with the tingling in his limbs and heart.

He wasn't sure where he was. Looking around, he saw a large, dimly lit room adorned with two-story-high statues. From his right, he noticed a soft crimson glow.

"Think," he whispered. "Try to remember."

He concentrated—and it all came back to him. He had been in gym class, having about as normal a day as he could have ever since his unexpected trip to the Early Cretaceous and back. Then the M.I.N.D. Machine had been activated, and once again things got crazy for Will. Only this time he'd stayed where he was and the "normal" world went haywire.

Dinosaurs had entered his junior high school. Real dinosaurs.

Will *knew* dinosaurs. He'd understood them ever since his conscious mind had been catapulted into the past by Bertram Phillips's M.I.N.D. Machine. For a time Will had actually lived in the scaly skin of a raptor. And when he had finally returned to the present, he'd realized that he hadn't made the journey alone. Another presence lived within him now, a fierce and honor-bound Acrocanthosaurus whom his girlfriend, Patience McCray, had named the Green Knight—G.K.,for short.

Will knew what dinosaurs smelled like. He knew what it was to stare one in the eye. He also knew that the dinosaurs that had been brought to his school weren't typical dinosaurs.

These dinosaurs had been shooting hoops in the gym. Racing around in the halls. Wandering, mumbling, and generally trying to understand what had happened to them.

These dinosaurs had the minds of sixth-, seventh-, and eighth-graders inside them.

And a handful of them had been after him.

"He's the only one who can stop it," an angry raptor had yelled as Will had hurled himself out the window of Wetherford Junior High, leaping into a dark, swirling void.

Then he had been falling, and now he was in this very large room—some kind of theater or auditorium.

Suddenly a curtain was yanked open and a blinding shaft of sunlight fell on Will. He scrambled back away from the light and stumbled into a darkened corner.

A figure approached. At first Will thought the figure was another dinosaur. Then it stopped in the pool of light and stared down at him.

What was looking his way wasn't a dinosaur. Not exactly.

"I say, are you lost?" the figure asked.

Will stared at the strange being who had spoken. It had a saurian snout, green and pink scales, tiny teeth, and an almost human-looking skull. It wore a red robe adorned with an elegant black pattern, and black cushioned sandals protected the soles of its feet.

"Should I send for someone?" the maybe-kinda-sorta dinosaur said. "Do you need help?"

Will heard a series of cluckings, chirps, and low vibrating growls accompanying the words. He sensed that he really didn't understand this being's language. Instead, the energies of the M.I.N.D. Machine were letting Will glimpse its thoughts and understand its intent.

Will sniffed. The creature smelled like a dinosaur. But Will could also detect the distinct scent of roses and jasmine.

The dinosaur *bathed* and used *fragrances*.

He looked around anxiously, wondering if he could outrun it if that became necessary. He didn't sense any harmful intent coming from the saurian— just the opposite, in fact. But the creature's presence was so odd to Will that it made him want to run.

This thing wasn't natural in the truest sense of the word. It was not of nature as Will understood it. Will's human and dinosaur senses firmly assured him that this creature did not belong in Will's world.

Or *maybe* it was the other way around.

Will sat in a shadow-laden corner of a great marble chamber. Sunlight glinted off amber statues of dinosaur warriors, philosophers, and statesmen. Heavy curtains were thrown over four of the five arched windows in the vast room. The creature who had found Will stood in a pool of sunlight. Will guessed that it was some kind of custodian.

"I'm all right," Will said, wondering if the robed saurian could understand his words.

The being took a step back. Will saw that the saurian's tail was very short. And unlike any dinosaur Will had ever seen, it stood with its back almost perfectly straight, very much like a human being.

"All right, you say? Well, I'm not sure that you are," the robed dinosaur said. "Why don't you step into the light, where I can see you?"

Will's instincts flared. He felt certain that letting

the saurian see him would be a terrible mistake. His nose itched, and he scratched it without thinking, his pale, five-fingered hand moving into the light.

The saurian gasped, and Will drew back his hand.

"You poor fellow," the saurian said, raising its own hands. They were scaly, but the nails were very small. *And* the creature had opposable thumbs. "You're suffering from some kind of skin condition, aren't you? Don't you have any friends? Anywhere you can go? A doctor, perhaps?"

Will thought of the void he had passed through to get here. He pressed his hand against the wall behind him.

It was solid.

"Nowhere," Will said. "I don't have anywhere I can go."

The saurian shook its head. "Well, I'm not sure how you got in here. But as much as I sympathize with your wanting to hide yourself away and avoid the stares your condition must bring, you cannot stay here. If you will wait a moment, I will look for something that might help."

Will watched as the saurian shimmied off. The robed figure left by a door at the far end of the room. Will waited until he heard the saurian's footsteps dwindle to nothingness. Then he rose and walked to the nearest of the curtained windows. Steeling himself, he brushed the curtain aside.

Blinding sunlight washed over him. He squinted and wished he had his mirrored shades. Then the buildings and the dwellings beyond the window took form. He looked onto a street that was incredibly wide. Dinosaurs—or things that looked as though they had evolved from dinosaurs—went past in either direction. The dinosaurs were all shapes and sizes. They wore cloaks and jewelry. Many were followed by floating disks containing bags or bits of machinery.

Will thought he might faint. He leaned against the window, expecting to feel glass. Instead, there was a hum, and a vibrating field of energy thrummed against him. He jumped back.

Technology!

They had *technology*.

This place was unlike any he had ever known. Carved into the towering buildings across the street he saw outdoor eateries, playgrounds, and what might have been schools. Craning his neck, he saw a two-hundred-foot-tall Sequoiadendron thriving between a pair of beautiful stone and steel edifices.

The sky was rich and blue, with soft white clouds and the barest hint of a misshapen pale object that might have been the moon if it had been perfectly round. Instead, it looked as if someone had taken a bite out of it.

It was all stunning.

A vast shape suddenly drifted past Will's window: a floating transport bearing dozens of tiny dinosaurs. The dinosaurs' eyes went wide at the sight of Will. He drew back and let the curtain fall into place as footsteps came from the hall. Will darted back to the shadows and stood quietly as the custodian entered. It carried a dark blue robe.

"Here," the custodian said. "I have no wish to make you uncomfortable. I'll leave this beside the statue of Shoolin Goth." The saurian laid the cloth over the arm of one of the carved amber statues. "I think he was the finest of our philosophers and deserves a place in the Great Hall, but I am seemingly alone in my belief. Ah, well, I must prepare the hall for visitors."

"I'll be quick," Will said.

"Good, yes. Kindness is welcome."

"Kindness is welcome," Will repeated automatically.

The custodian shimmied away.

Will left the shadows and slipped the robe on. It had a hood, which he pulled up over his head. The robe was a bit too long, but as long as he was careful, he wouldn't trip over the excess fabric.

Okay, he thought, *this is great. Here I am, I'm alone, dinos rule. How do I get back?*

Will felt a familiar tug deep in the core of his

being, a pull toward something that offered comfort, familiarity—and possibly escape.

The M.I.N.D. Machine was calling him.

Will darted from the hall. He hurried along an empty corridor and navigated a spiral staircase with tall, flat steps that were not made for human feet.

At the foot of the stairs he saw a door bursting with sunlight. Murmurs drifted to him from deeper within the gallery, and he sped away, toward the light. A figure appeared in the doorway, a tall creature with a long neck and a two-foot-long jaw.

"Slow down, small one," the long-neck said. "Kindness is welcome!"

"Yes, I'm sorry," Will said. He kept the hood low and looked away, hoping the shadows would prevent the dinosaur from seeing his face.

"What did you say?" the long-neck asked. "I don't understand."

Will glanced up. The long-neck had a small tail and a straight spine, like the other saurian. "I said I'm sorry. I apologized."

The creature stared at him blankly.

"Sorry," Will said. "Sorrow. I expressed sorrow."

"Sorrow," the long-neck repeated. "What an odd word. What does it mean?"

Will didn't know what to say. "I'm—I'm late!"

He slipped past the ten-foot-tall saurian.

"Late," the long-neck muttered. "Another strange

word. Ah, the young ones like to make new words, I suppose..."

Will slipped through a crowd of dinosaurs and nearly stumbled as he stepped onto the moving sidewalk. A robed saurian steadied him.

"Kindness is welcome," Will said.

"Oh, yes," the saurian said. It looked as if it had descended from a Troodon. "Especially in these unusual times."

With a hop, the saurian transferred to the other half of the moving road and sailed away in the opposite direction.

Unusual times? Will thought. He wondered what the saurian was talking about. He stayed close behind a collection of upright-walking dinosaurs, drawing his cloak tightly around him. There was a mild chill in the air. He listened to some of the saurians as the moving roadway took him toward the M.I.N.D. Machine. Will felt the warmth within him grow as he approached its location.

"I planned to go to the Antiquarian's Aquarium today to see De'Loth, my adviser," said the nearest of the saurians. He looked as though he might be a Deinonychus, a raptor, but there was only a small knob on his feet where his retractable sickle claws should have been.

"The swimmer? I didn't know he was visiting from the great sea," replied another declawed raptor.

"I quite enjoy the conversation of dolphins," the first raptor said. "But I was told this morning that the aquarium has vanished."

"The Vanishing, yes," his companion said. "Very unusual. It is taking place in all the great cities. One moment a place is there, the next—"

Will heard a cry of alarm and looked up. A dark, swirling void had appeared a hundred yards ahead. It was swallowing up everyone and everything on the great moving road!

For an instant Will wondered if this vortex might take him home. Then he felt a chill where the warm tug from the M.I.N.D. Machine had been, and he sensed that it would take him somewhere he might not want to go.

Ahead, several dinosaurs scurried off the road and onto the crowded sidewalk, while others simply stared at the unusual phenomenon and allowed themselves to be swallowed whole.

"Interesting," the first raptor said. "Perhaps I will see De'Loth after all."

Will couldn't believe what he was hearing. Didn't these creatures understand the danger they were in? The vortex might take them *anywhere,* yet they weren't at all concerned.

Will leaped to safety as the raptors slid into the hungry void. He fell to the ground and was immediately helped by a pair of three-foot-high saurians. Microvenators, from the look of their long arms, though they had no claws.

When he turned back to the road, the vortex was gone.

Is this my fault? Will wondered. *Did I bring that thing here?*

He had no answers.

"Kindness is welcome," he said, pulling his cloak down and stepping away from the Microvenators. He walked along the sidewalk, passing an outdoor eatery. A saurian went to a table and gestured, and a stream of clear, fresh water rose and flowed right to his maw.

With another gesture, the saurian brought a huge bowl filled with fresh greens into existence. Another bowl held grinding stones to help with digestion.

Will watched the scene in awe.

Further down the street, he peered into buildings and saw saurians bring clothing, jewelry, and more into existence. He listened as saurians discussed philosophy and art.

All the time, he felt the pull of the machine grow stronger.

Finally he stopped before a building made of crystal. Beautiful pastel colors flowed through the entrance portal.

The M.I.N.D. Machine was in here. Will could feel it.

He stepped through the portal, and a huge dinosaur with a spike reaching up from its snout stepped before him.

"This is a place of solitude and contemplation, young one," the dinosaur said. "If you wish to play, there are many other places."

Solitude and contemplation, Will thought. *Like a science lab.*

Will had to get inside. He drew his cloak back and let the dinosaur see his human face.

The saurian gasped and passed out. Its huge form struck the floor with only a soft thud. The floor melted and molded itself to cushion the dinosaur's fall.

Will had meant only to surprise the dinosaur so that he could run past it. He hoped the saurian would be all right.

Inside the crystal portal Will was faced with a honeycomb of tunnels. It reminded him of the mountain he had been trapped within when he had been in the Early Cretaceous. He didn't have to put a lot of effort into choosing the way to go. The warmth he felt deep inside was becoming an inferno, and the pull toward the machine nearly dragged him off his feet.

He passed through tunnels, darting beyond rooms filled with soft-spoken saurians.

Each spoke of the Vanishings—and the void.

No one had any idea what was happening.

The last corridor turned sharply to the left, then ended abruptly. A darkened chamber lit only by flickering blue-white light lay directly ahead.

The machine was there.

Will pulled his cloak tightly around him and entered the chamber.

The machine was exactly as he remembered it. The long side panels shone brightly with sparkling energies, and the monitors were alive with a host of strange images. The images were *all* of people. Human beings.

A lone saurian stood near the machine. It wore a white robe with silver and blue trim. It had a long neck and a curling tail. Its brow was furrowed, and it looked deep in thought.

"Yes, come in. I've been expecting you," the saurian said.

Will took a few steps closer to the machine—and the scientist examining it.

"The artifact was unearthed a little over a week ago," the saurian said. It stared at the images of people playing sports, laughing, kissing, and walking on the moon. "It had been swept out to sea along with volcanic rock that dates at approximately one hundred and fifty million years in age. It should have been melted to slag, but as you can see, it has been perfectly preserved."

Will nodded. He looked to see if the machine was plugged into some kind of energy source. It wasn't. The machine seemed to be running itself.

"My theory is that this machine is unraveling our reality," the scientist said. "And that you may be the only one who can help to stop it."

Will was startled. The raptors who had tried to keep him from escaping Wetherford had said almost exactly the same thing.

Waiting until the scientist was looking his way, Will pulled back the hood of his cloak. The scientist's shoulders slumped in relief.

"It is you," the scientist said. Its head bobbed on its long neck as it spoke. "You are the one I have seen in my dreams. Will Reilly. That is your name."

"Yeah," Will said.

The scientist's leathery lips pulled back in a soft smile. "You are the logical choice to be the walker between our worlds. You are more than human. There is another spirit within you. A saurian spirit."

Will nodded again.

"Then allow me to introduce myself properly," the scientist said.

"I know who you are," Will said. "There's only one person you can be. Bertram."

The scientist looked puzzled. "No. My name is Jae'Dee. Jae'Dee Harms. And this place, if you didn't already guess, is the Dinoverse."

CHAPTER 6

BERTRAM

Bertram teetered on his feet as he slowly awoke from his trancelike state.

For a brief time he had been looking out through Will's eyes, seeing and feeling everything his friend had experienced. Now, however, that reality was slowly fading, although the crackling blue-white lightning still surrounded him and a voice continued to speak to him through the wind. It was Will's voice.

"I worked on the machine with the saurians. And I think we've learned about as much as we're going to. There's no saying exactly what the Dinoverse is. Jae'Dee says it could be a separate but divergent reality from our own. In other words, for every life-changing choice we make or action we take that changes our world, there is another reality that exists—the same as the one we knew, only without that one action or decision that changed everything."

Bertram understood the theory. He nervously waited for Will to continue.

"This Dinoverse is a good place. These are good creatures. But their reality is fading. I think ours is, too. Bertram, according to what we can learn from the M.I.N.D. Machine, it all goes back to where you are now and what you may or may not do there in the past. Their past, our past—they seem to be the same...at least until you and the other students arrived."

Bertram closed his eyes as Will's words sank in. In some future reality, human evolution had been swapped for a Dinoverse. And it was all because of something he and the other students had done—or would do—back here.

"I'm sorry to have to tell you this, Bertram. There's no easy way of doing it, and I wish I didn't have to. But you have to fix things. You have to get the machine working again, and you have to set everything back the way it was. There isn't a lot of time, either. In two days the volcano with the jagged peak is going to blow. You have to get everyone out of the valley before that happens. You have to get the machine to safety, too. And you have to make things right."

Bertram shuddered. It was all up to him.

"Just remember, Bertram, we're all connected.

*Everyone and everything is connected. And
nothing happens without a reason. Nothing.
Figure out the reason for all of this, and you'll
figure out what to do to make things right."*

Bertram heard the wind dying down. He saw the
crackling lightning fade. "Will, wait! You have to tell
me more, show me more!"

But the wind and lightning vanished, leaving
Bertram to stare out at the ash-colored sky and think
about all he had seen and heard.

For about five seconds.

"That was wicked," Aaron said. "I mean that
place, the Dinoverse. Seeing it and walking around in
it like your buddy Will. Very cool."

Bertram was both stunned and overwhelmed with
the desire to snap at his brother and perhaps even
give him a little warning bite on the shoulder. His
strange new predator instincts were flaring once more.

"You saw all that?" Bertram asked.

Aaron nodded.

Bertram looked down from the rise into the valley
of dinosaurs. Every one of them looked the way he
felt, as if they were drifting out of thick mental fogs.

The memories Will had downloaded into Bertram's
mind hadn't gone just to him. Bertram now realized
that everyone had seen. Everyone had heard.

One by one the dinosaurs in the valley looked to
Bertram. They looked frightened.

"You can make it work again," one of the spike-tailed Stegosaurus said anxiously. "You can do that, right?"

"I think so," Bertram said.

The scissor-jawed predator shouted, "Louder, Bertram! We can't hear you! Project!"

Project? Bertram thought. *Isn't that an acting term? Strange that Holly would use such a word.*

He cleared his throat and started walking down the rise, Aaron at his side.

"We've got a plan," Bertram said. He studied the odd collection of dinosaurs around him. From the map Will had downloaded into his head, he knew that they were in Beverly Hills, 150 million years in the past. And some of the dinosaurs he saw fit pretty well into what he knew of that area and that time.

But others didn't belong here at all.

It was just like what Will had seen in the Dinoverse, a crazy mix of dinosaur species from every region of the globe—and every period of the 200-million-year span known as the Mesozoic, the age of dinosaurs.

The one thing Bertram knew for sure, from his past studies of the fossil record, was that while they were in a location that might one day be a posh Beverly Hills address, much of the actual soil they were now standing upon would ultimately be swept into the western sea by floods or picked up and carried away to the eastern flats by incredible storms.

These floods and storms could easily hit at the exact same moment—or even sooner—as the volcanic eruption that he knew was soon to arrive. Either way, the inevitable climate forecast didn't bode well for any of them.

"What's the plan?" the scissor-jaw asked.

"I know I said I had a plan," Bertram said uncertainly. "But with what Will told us about the volcano—"

Aaron clamped one claw on Bertram's shoulder. "We have to move the machine to higher ground—get it and all the rest of us to safety before the eruption. Then we can worry about making it work."

Bertram again felt an odd mixture of admiration and annoyance. Once again Aaron had come up with a simple, straightforward plan while he was stumbling around, trying to navigate through subtle and complex factors.

"Yeah, that's right," Bertram said. "But there's one thing that's going to be crucial over the next couple of days."

"That we don't panic?" a girl in a Compsognathus body asked.

"Make that two things," Bertram said. He raised his snout, feeling just a little more confident in the role of leader that had apparently been thrust on him. Then he noticed something. "The Apatosaurus! Where'd he go?"

The spike-tails glanced at each other, then looked around. "J.D. took off! Cool!"

"Not cool," Bertram said as he finished walking down the rise and into the midst of the group. "Not cool at all. And here's why."

CHAPTER 7

J.D.

J.D. Harms had never run from anything in his life. He also didn't stay around when he wasn't wanted or needed. Or when he just didn't like a place.

Now he was hiking around the foothills of a volcano, far from the crowd of losers and their weird visions and problems. The sight of Jae'Dee Harms—the soft-spoken dinosaur that was supposed to be *him* in the other reality—had been all he could take. He had gotten out of there while the others were trying to get themselves together.

This body was weak. The dinosaur he inhabited was a coward. It had been all J.D. could do not to give in to the fear his host felt at being surrounded by predators and the angry spike-tails.

When he had first found himself in the age of dinosaurs, he had been ecstatic. Back in Wetherford, his favorite thing in the world was heading into the mountains with a backpack and losing himself there for the weekend. He hated being around people. Hated *needing* things from them.

But the body that he was in—a pudgy little long-neck—wasn't exactly what he'd had in mind. Or what his dreams had promised.

And the other J.D. had been having dreams, too...

J.D. started climbing. His parents worried when he went off by himself. They worried about everything. And despite what everyone thought, J.D. didn't really like making them worry.

Well...not his mom, anyway. His *dad* could worry all he wanted. After all that man had put them through, a little worry was what he deserved. Maybe even a *lot*.

J.D. cautiously surveyed the area. He knew there were predators around, predators who were nothing but meat-eaters. Carnivores.

He almost felt he had a better chance against them than the ones who had eighth-graders within their scaly hides. Having a history with people sometimes made things tough, though he honestly couldn't remember either of the kids who had attacked him—the ones now in the bodies of spike-tailed Stegosaurus.

All those kids he had trashed in the halls or outside the school were just object lessons. It was his way of telling people to stay away from him—or else.

His life had been simple before. It would be simple again.

The first thing he wanted to do was find a safe and defensible area. That meant getting to higher ground.

Climbing wasn't easy in his new elephantine body. He was used to having muscle to back up his bulk, not flab. He couldn't leap up the terraces he had seen along the bases of other volcanoes.

Some of the volcanoes had flat shelves stretching around their bases, and he could navigate through these easily. Several miles back, J.D. had spotted the volcano that was going to blow, and he had looked for signs of other volcanoes that were dormant: no warmth coming from them, no fissures spouting scalding steam, stone that was lighter-colored and not charred black.

Some of the mountains that *might* have held volcanoes were dotted with deep hollows and caves. These were surrounded by tons of fresh greens.

He was starved. His body was telling him that it would be happy if he did nothing but stand still, eat, find more food, eat, take a nap, and then eat.

"I'm putting you on a diet, lardo," J.D. muttered.

J.D. was on a quest to find his own place, and he had no intention of eating until he settled on one. He decided that if he were a predator looking to munch down on a long-neck, the first thing he would do is look for areas that had been lush with vegetation and were now picked clean. So he would find one place to live and other places to eat.

He'd keep 'em guessing, just like old Trapp used to tell him.

Joseph Trapp was a naturalist who lived off the land and made his own clothing. He also made his own way through life. Trapp was a confessed former suit who had "seen the way."

I know the way out of all of this, son, Trapp would tell him when they ran into each other in the mountains outside Wetherford. *Just turn your back and walk away. It doesn't have to be any more complicated than that.*

J.D. couldn't exactly call Trapp a friend. That would be like admitting he needed someone. But he certainly admired the man.

When you're out in the open where predators might be huntin', you've got to be careful to cover your tracks and watch where you leave your scent and your spoor, Trapp had explained to him. With that in mind, eating was going to have to wait, no matter how run-down and light-headed he felt.

J.D. checked the direction of the wind again. He wanted to make sure no predator would catch his scent.

He had done this five times in the last ten minutes.

Maybe he was a little edgy.

He thought of the past that had been promised to him in his dreams. His time as tyrant king, a predator with no concerns.

Instead, that little dweeb Bertram and scissor-jawed Holly had gotten the good bodies. Even those two jerks with the armor and spiked tails were better off than he was.

You make do with what you got. That's what Trapp would tell him.

Well, he might be slow, but at least he was strong. Look at how he had knocked that other scissor-jawed predator down that hill!

J.D. scanned around until he saw a plateau. It looked high enough to escape the coming volcanic eruption. And it would be safe from predators, too.

Ringed in by high stone walls on every side but one, the path leading up to the plateau was a steep climb, and it was just wide enough for him to fit through, which meant that any large predators would have to approach single file.

J.D. slowly climbed the path and saw that there were plenty of boulders lying around at the top that he could roll down onto any unwelcome visitors. This place was perfect!

Now he could go get some grub.

J.D. had to be careful as he walked back down the path from his new home. His front legs slid, and he worried that he might go tumbling end over end if he made a single misstep. That thought made him very happy, because if it was this hard for him, it would be just as difficult for the larger predators he had seen. Maybe even impossible. A perfect fortress!

When J.D. made it to the base of his stronghold, he looked around and spotted a green area a mile away, closer to the shore. *Munch time.*

No other dinosaurs crossed J.D.'s path as he made his way to the feeding ground. He was leaving tracks, but that couldn't be avoided. Eventually he'd work out some way of covering his tracks. For now, though, his belly was firmly in control. He had never wanted to chow down on a salad so badly in his life!

J.D. reached a dense forest of ferns, conifers, and cycads and stopped before a magnificent, towering pine tree at least two hundred feet high. He put his hunger aside and gazed at the tree as he might have in the wilds of Montana.

Awe washed over him as he stood in the tree's presence. The tree's limbs and roots were strong. It stood separate and defiant, satisfied with its solitary state. The tree had been there for hundreds of years, and it would stand for hundreds more. It didn't need anyone or anything. J.D. felt honored to stand in its presence.

This would be a good life after all.

Of course, he'd miss a few things. Like his books. There would be no Hemingway, Updike, or Faulkner in this land, and he would never have the pleasure of sinking his teeth into a nice juicy steak with extra onions—but he figured that was a small sacrifice, a reasonable trade.

J.D. turned from the tree and mashed his face into a collection of low-lying ferns. As he gobbled them up, his attention became less focused. He felt overwhelmed now by the sheer pleasure of filling his belly, of moving from one mass of leaves to another.

As he ate, J.D. even lost track of time—until he heard the first of the low roars in the distance. The sounds startled him back to reality.

Time to go.

The roars had come from the shoreline, and the wind was blowing from that direction, which meant the predators wouldn't be able to smell him. *Good.*

Then he heard roars from the *opposite* direction. The dinosaurs making those sounds would be able to scent him, J.D. realized at once.

He considered making a run for it, but he knew how slow this body was and how much noise it would make blundering over the uneven ground.

Scanning the area, J.D. searched for a refuge. He'd never make his plateau fortress, so he'd have to find another—maybe a cave that was just big enough for him, but not for any of the larger predators. He'd have to show these guys that going after him would be a waste of time and effort. There was easier prey out there—such as a couple of spike-tailed dinos he knew.

He wouldn't be running or hiding, he told himself. He'd just be playing it smart.

Footfalls sounded from deep within the forest. They were soft, and the ground trembled only a little. But in seconds the footfalls became thunderous, the roars accompanying them deafening.

J.D. froze as the towering tree he had admired was smashed to toothpicks by another of the scissor-jaws. The predator advanced on him with terrifying speed. J.D. couldn't bring himself to move.

The predator roared—then yelped as it tripped over the jagged stump of the tree that it had just destroyed. It fell facedown on one of the shattered branches.

J.D. rose and balanced on his hind legs, a pitiful squeal coming from his throat. His body's instinctual reaction enraged him.

Then he noticed the tracks he had left in the earth and the nasty claws at the end of his tree-trunk-sized front paws. Just as the scissor-jaw was about to rise, J.D. pounced on the dinosaur. He beat and clawed at the predator, avoiding its snapping maw. Then he backed up and kicked it in the face.

The predator sank into unconsciousness, its nostrils fluttering.

J.D. turned and ran. He moved at a trot, slamming into branches and kicking up heavy stones. He made more noise than he wanted to, but right now all that mattered was reaching safety.

The roars came from all directions. Obviously the scissor-jaws hunted in packs!

J.D. saw a rock-covered hill a few hundred yards away. It wasn't as perfectly defensible as the place he had chosen to call home, but he judged that he could make it there before the predators could reach him. At least it was higher ground, and from up there he could use his tail to send rocks flying down at his enemies.

He ran faster, hating that he couldn't just stand and fight. But he knew this was a battle he couldn't win.

Footfalls came again. Roars sounded from behind him and off to the right. The predators were close. He wasn't going to make it to the hill!

Near the base of a volcano, he saw a series of deep, long niches carved into the earth. They looked like trenches soldiers might have dug in wartime. One was about thirty feet deep and a hundred feet long. It spilled out near the base of the hill J.D. wanted to reach.

J.D. saw one of the scissor-jaws appear close to his flank as he raced for the trench. He leaped over the edge of the trench, the snap of a hungry, angry dinosaur hanging in the air. J.D.'s heavy body landed at the bottom of the trench with an explosive thud. He stumbled, then scurried in as deep as he could.

Looking up, J.D. saw the scissor-jaws watching him from a dozen feet up. Their bodies were too wide to fit into the trench. If they tried, they would be trapped, and they were apparently smart enough to know that much.

Great!

One of the predators bent over and leaned in, his snout reaching close enough to J.D.'s face for him to smell the animal's rancid breath. The predator's drool dripped onto J.D.'s brow as it snapped, growled, and roared in J.D.'s face—but it couldn't reach him.

Snap—snap snap—Rioooourrrggghhh!

Three of the ugly scissor-jaws gathered above. They kicked and stomped and snapped. One bounced up and down angrily. None of them could reach J.D. He had outmaneuvered them.

He had also gotten himself *trapped*.

J.D. had to think about this. What if these guys decided to camp out and wait for him? He couldn't stay in the trench forever. Not without food or water. He had to do something. But what?

There was only one way out, up a ramp made of earth and stone that lay at the far end of the trench.

One of the scissor-jaws stomped over to the way

out and squatted there. The predator looked as though he was smiling.

"Okay," J.D. said. His body was shaking. His inner dinosaur was such a wuss. But the truth was, the human part of him felt scared, too.

It had been a long time since J.D. had been scared of anything. Probably the last time had been at that Beverly Hills hospital when he'd stood at his mother's bedside, watching as the bandages came off from her reconstructive surgeries.

Her face looked almost the way it had before the accident, except that part of it was paralyzed. And always would be. She'd never be able to smile again. Or cry. No matter what she was feeling, her face would always be passive, serene. Like a mask.

That frightened him.

She had been a spirited person, alive and glowing with life. Now that was gone. Trapped within herself, she'd lost all joy. Her eyes were dark and sad. Her light had dimmed.

J.D.'s fear hadn't lasted. It had quickly turned to anger at his father—the one man who could have done more.

Being a doctor's son should have been an easy life, but it hadn't been for J.D. Until the accident, he'd gone to his father's office. He'd seen patients with him, admired him, learned things from him.

But J.D. had learned too much from his father.

He'd listened to his dad's patients as they gave excuses for not being able to pay their bills—yet they'd talk about the expensive vacations they took or the new things they'd gotten for their homes or their kids. And J.D. had stayed up late many nights waiting for his mother to come home from the part-time job that really paid their bills.

J.D. had learned that his father was weak. A soft, compassionate idiot who let everyone take advantage of him.

Dr. Harms's best buddy was a plastic surgeon in Beverly Hills. If not for that guy, who knew what J.D.'s mom would look like today. But it had cost them. Friend or not, the massive bills for all the surgeries had come in one day.

"Hey, Josh, come on, join the practice, move to Beverly Hills," his father's friend had said. "You'll make a fortune and pay this off in no time. You have to be a specialist. Do *one* thing. General practitioners are like dinosaurs today."

At home J.D. felt helpless—and trapped.

He could do nothing to help either of his parents. And they were too lost in their own struggles to notice him or what he needed. So he decided not to need anymore.

He'd done all he could to get free of the suffocating downward spiral, carving his own identity, forging a mask no one could look beyond.

He would never be trapped again.

Hollering wildly, J.D. ran at the predator waiting for him at the end of the trench.

If you have to fight someone, attack them on their strengths, not their weaknesses, Trapp had told him. *Go right up the center and take them where they won't be expecting it.*

The scissor-jaw at the entrance rose excitedly, his claws clicking, his body jittery with anticipation.

J.D. ran, all too aware of the sounds coming from his own dinosaur body. Soft, high bleatings pierced the air—and something inside him made him trip over his own feet. He tumbled to the ground as the scissor-jaw's face rushed toward him, teeth snapping. It couldn't reach him.

J.D. lay on the ground on his side, crying and shuddering, unable to control himself. He was caught. Helpless.

Alone.

Then he heard voices. Human voices. The scissor-jaw looked up and roared in warning. Other roars came in answer. The scissor-jaws all raced toward the noises. The earth shuddered as roars and screams and thuds sounded. For a very long time it sounded like a war was being fought, and J.D. couldn't bring himself to move.

Finally the sounds of battle died away and voices came again. Cheering, victorious voices.

J.D. was on his feet by the time Bertram and the others arrived.

"I've been through this before," Bertram said. "There's only one way to make it out. Either we all go back or no one goes back. We stay together."

J.D. said nothing. He raised his head and did his best to look nonchalant as he walked out of the trench.

"You could say thanks," another dinosaur said, its dual crests quivering in the mild breeze.

J.D. knew that voice. It was the slacker. That little weasel Aaron!

J.D. walked up to Aaron—and head-butted the dweeb.

"Ow!" Aaron yelled.

With a laugh, J.D. walked away. Maybe this place had possibilities after all.

PART TWO
JURASSIC JAM

CHAPTER 8

CLAIRE

Claire dreamed that she was on yet another in an endless series of auditions. Only this time when she was asked to read, the part she was auditioning for was herself. She would be playing Claire DeLacey!

Even though she put her heart into the audition, the casting agents simply shook their heads.

"Not convincing," a woman in a dark business suit said from across a wide desk. "Crystal Claire is dainty and sweet."

A young guy in a designer suit leaned forward. "We just don't think you grasp the inner workings of this character. Do you have any idea what she wants? Or how far she'd go to get it?"

Claire tried to answer the casting director's questions, but he wouldn't listen. The other casting people shook their heads and studied other résumés. One of them got up and turned on a radio. Wild fifties beach blanket music swelled around her.

Her mom had been in, like, a *dozen* of those flicks

105

when she was a teenager.

"Make it stop," Claire groaned. She shook herself awake, but the music did not stop. Looking down, she saw that she was still in the body of the scissor-jawed predator. The past was real and all around her.

Strangely, that knowledge was a comfort.

"Hey, Holly, come on and dance!" Melissa called.

Claire surveyed the beach. Everywhere she looked, dinosaurs were getting down. Melissa waved frantically as she danced.

The ground thumped and thundered. Tails wagged and slapped. Hearty growls and laughing yips filled the air as scaly, brilliantly colored dinosaurs hopped and shook their booty.

Claire thought of Bertram's stories. In them, at least one student always developed advanced psychic powers, including the ability to project sights and sounds from his or her memory.

"Go, Reggie, go!" someone cried.

Claire sighed as she saw the obnoxious Reggie holding a stick as though it were a microphone.

"All right, and welcome, everyone, to the first annual Jurassic Jam!" Reggie hollered. "Boss man's away, so that means it's time for all good dinosaurs to play!"

Claire noticed that Bertram was nowhere in sight. He was probably off working on the machine.

She sighed and considered reminding everyone

that they were supposed to be working in shifts. A new day had come, and there was a lot to do.

But that was what *Claire* would say and do.

Holly, on the other hand—the girl they all believed her to be—would sit off to the side like J.D. and just shake her head at this bunch of losers.

So that was what she did. Not that she thought the others were losers or anything. But she had to maintain the role. If she didn't, then everyone would start treating her like Crystal Claire again, and it wouldn't matter what body she was in.

A wild holler of pure bliss sounded from the waves.

Claire nearly exploded with laughter at the sight of Aaron cresting the waves on a "surfboard" that was really just a slab of wood carved into the right shape.

The Dilophosaurus's dual wiggly crests fluttered in the breeze, and he struck a pose that looked straight out of *Baywatch* or the cover of a surfer magazine. The wave coming in was a big one, and Aaron was riding it for all it was worth!

"Go for it, Moondoggie!" Reggie yelled.

Claire stood and studied Aaron's expression. He looked intense, perfectly focused, and blissfully removed from any and every possible concern. The only time she had felt like that was when she was acting.

So what are you waiting for? her agent whispered in her mind. *You've got a character to play. Play it!*

Claire tried to remember the way Holly Cronk walked. She moved as though there were a beat nearby that only she could hear. Not quite a bounce in her step, but more of a hip-hop groove.

She walked over to Melissa, and they stared at Reggie.

"'Sup?" Claire asked. She had rarely heard Holly speak. Not much to go on, really, but she figured the eighth-grader would round off "what's up" to "'sup."

Melissa looked at her strangely. She didn't seem to get it.

With a sigh, Claire nodded in Reggie's direction. "That guy never learns, does he? He just has to be the center of attention."

"Got that right," Melissa said.

Claire frowned inwardly. Holly wouldn't talk so much. That was one of *Claire's* traits. Something she did when she was nervous.

"But I think that Aaron guy's cool," Melissa said.

Claire and Melissa watched as Aaron got to the shore, shook himself, and waddled back into the waves with his board. He had to belly-flop onto the board, get his legs under himself, and push off with his little arms. Claire was astonished by the display. This guy was *born* to the waves, no doubt about it. His sense of balance was stunning.

"I can't imagine what this must be like for him," Melissa said in a sympathetic voice. "Here he is on his first day at a new school, and first that jerk J.D. picks on him, then Crystal Claire freezes him out, then he gets zapped by Bertram's machine. At least the rest of us were kind of used to weird things happening at Wetherford—"

"What'd you say?" Claire asked. Her tail stiffened, and her eyes narrowed.

Melissa appeared too taken with the sight of Aaron on the surfboard to notice the change in Claire's stance. "You know, with the stories and all, and the actual machine, and—I dunno, it almost feels natural being back here. For us, I mean."

"No, about *Claire*. I didn't hear anything about her shutting him down."

Melissa shrugged. "Just talk. Y'know. Everyone was saying he had a thing for her, but she wouldn't even talk to him."

She had a vague memory of Aaron walking her way before the M.I.N.D. Machine zapped them. But J.D. had intercepted him, and then someone had ushered her to "safety."

"I'm gonna make that boy forget all about little Miss Priss," Melissa said.

Claire worked out the kinks in her neck. Little bones popped. "So you don't much like Claire, is that it?"

"She's all right," Melissa said. "If you go for that whole 'Oh, I'm following my dream, and don't touch me, and I'm better than everyone' kind of thing. You know."

Claire took another step. Towering over Melissa, she opened her maw and felt saliva drip down. "Really?"

Melissa swatted at the top of her head as if it had started raining. She still wouldn't take her gaze off Aaron. "Yeah. I can just imagine poor Aaron trying to talk to her. 'Hey, Claire, how about pizza and a movie?'"

"That's romantic, sure," Claire said. The throbbing music was starting to grate on her nerves, and she was shifting her weight from one foot to the other, a hazy red cloud of fury drifting up from her angry inner dinosaur. "And how would Claire react?"

Melissa reared up on her hind legs and set her hands as delicately near her hips as possible. "She'd probably go, 'Oh, but you're too close to my aura, it's going to change color, eeeewww!'"

Claire felt a low rumble rising from within her.

"Was that your stomach?" Melissa asked. "You should really get something to eat!"

You're Holly Cronk, Holly Cronk, Holly Cronk, Claire chanted in her mind. *Just stay cool, keep it under control.*

"Hey, check it out!" Reggie yelled. "Surfer dude's got company!"

Claire left Melissa's side and walked to the water's edge. A whole school of sleek steel-gray forms swam around Aaron.

"Dolphins," Claire said, unable to hide her natural excitement and wonder. *"Dolphins!"*

Cruising over the waves, Aaron nodded to the seven-foot-long shapes. Then one flew from the waters, revealing a long, thin snout filled with razor-sharp teeth! It snapped at Aaron, and he nearly fell from his surfboard. Others jumped from the water, one sinking its teeth into the wood slab he'd been riding. The dolphin-shark twisted fiercely, its huge, bloated belly flopping out of the water, and Aaron was thrown off balance and into the sea!

The water quickly swallowed him, and the dophin-sharks dove beneath the blue to follow him. Behind Claire, Melissa screamed.

The music stopped. Everyone froze.

Melissa ran up to Claire. "Do something!"

Claire had no idea what to do. She saw fins and wriggling tails descend into the depths.

"W-well, um," Claire stammered, "someone's got to get in there, um, if I went in, the, ah, sand, it might, y'know, like quicksand, I—"

Suddenly Bertram was rushing down the rise. "Temnodontosaurus! Those things are meat-eaters! Holly, help him!"

She spun, her tail nearly knocking down Melissa. "But—"

"The ash in the sky is from a recent eruption," Bertram hollered. "Lava flowed into the water and cooled, hardening. Get in there, you won't sink!"

Claire looked down and realized it wasn't sand she had been sleeping on—it was volcanic ash.

She rushed forward. *Holly is brave, Holly is strong, Holly doesn't need anyone protecting her.*

As she plunged into the warm water, she saw a handful of the snapping dolphin-sharks turn from Aaron and sail her way.

Holly is gonna get eaten.

She hesitated, floundering in the waters, staring at the approaching Temnodontosaurus. Their eyes were gleeful.

Flipper's gone psycho, Claire thought. *This is crazy. I shouldn't be doing my own stunts—*

Then the first was on her. She turned her head so fast that her own scissor jaw smashed the predator's face, sending it reeling away. Another opened its mouth to take a bite just as Claire fell over. Her claws stabbed into the predator's side as she sank beneath the waters.

Bubbles rose as she gasped and panicked and tried to get to her feet. With a grunt she brained the dolphin-shark by slapping it onto the bottom. Then she tripped and fell again, spinning in the waters.

You're Holly Cronk! she thought. *What are you gonna do? Cry? Come on!*

She wanted to cry. She felt as though she was going to drown, as though she had no idea what to do next.

Then a dolphin-shark snapped at her tail. Her instincts coupled with her rage and frustration as she bounced in the water, landing on her feet. She opened her jaws wide and bit into the smooth belly of the predator.

Her mind exploded with crimson and heat. For the next few moments she had virtually no idea what she was doing. Then she burst from the water, gulped in air, and submerged once again, half swimming, half hopping on the ocean's floor, searching for anything that might satisfy her hunger.

Finally her senses cleared and she heard cheering. Bertram was swimming by, towing the dazed Aaron. Claire sank below the water, bounced back to the surface, and made her way to shore. Looking behind her, she realized that she had just had lunch. *Yuck.* But the other meat-eaters weren't complaining. They waded into the water and hungrily went after what was left of the dolphin-sharks.

Only one figure was waiting on the shore to greet her. The long-neck. J.D. He seemed to be smiling.

"Hey, *Holly,*" J.D. said. "I was thinking that you and me, we oughta talk."

CHAPTER 9

J.D.

J.D. led the other dinosaur away to a secluded arroyo as Bertram paced up and down the shore, lecturing the other students about the danger they faced and the responsibilities they carried.

"He sure can talk, can't he?" J.D. asked. "And did you get the bit about him and Aaron being *brothers*? Just right for a couple of dweebs like them. 'Course, it does make you think about family a little. I mean, look at the size of me. There's got to be others like me around here somewhere. Unless the other scissor-jaws like you got to them first."

He studied the dinosaur before him. She blinked slowly, with worry and regret, and looked away.

He had her.

"I bet those other guys who tried to eat me are your brothers," J.D. said. "That would explain why they're hanging around. You've got to feel something inside you that would let you know. Do you?"

The predator shuddered.

J.D. could only barely restrain a laugh of triumph. Finally he said, "Come on, *Claire,* 'fess up."

The scissor-jaw whirled on him. "I'm not—I mean, my name, um—"

"You're not Holly Cronk," J.D. said. "Don't bother trying to convince me that you are. It isn't gonna work."

The predator leaned over him, casting her huge, threatening shadow. J.D.'s inner dinosaur wanted to wimp out and run, but J.D. kept it under control, feeding it images of dainty little Crystal Claire running through a field of daisies.

His inner dino sighed and went back to sleep.

"Bertram said we all go back or none of us does," the predator said with a snarl. "He didn't say anything about all of us having to be in one piece."

J.D. smiled to himself. She was good, he had to give her that. "You know, we're a lot alike."

The towering dinosaur stopped, her brow crinkling. "How's that?"

"We both have to put on a show to get what we want, for one thing," J.D. said. "And neither of us likes having other people do things for us. But we're stuck."

The predator shook her head. "I'm not stuck at all. I can do whatever I want."

"Sure you can," J.D. said. "So long as everyone keeps thinking you're Holly."

The scissor-jaw was silent.

"Come on, Claire. I was watching the way you were acting. And I don't mean your behavior. I mean the performance. It was off. But I can help you with that. I can make it so no one suspects a thing."

"Really," the predator said flatly. Then she laughed. Her voice as Holly was deeper and grittier, but J.D. could hear the soft parts always trying to creep out. "Who'd listen to you, anyway?"

"They probably wouldn't believe me at first," J.D. said. "But do you really want them looking at you that closely? Do you really want them wondering?"

The massive predator looked to the sky. Her dark eyes closed slowly. Then, in Claire's soft voice, she said, "What gave me away?"

"Holly wouldn't have gone after that slacker," J.D. said. "And she wouldn't have jumped when Bertram gave her an order. Not a chance."

"You know her that well?"

"Well enough," J.D. said. In some ways what he was saying was true. Holly Cronk had no friends. She and J.D. had exchanged a dozen words total in their years at Wetherford. But when he looked in her eyes, he felt he understood her.

"I guess you want to know why I did it," Claire said.

"Couldn't care less. But I could use someone like

you watching my back. I've got a lot of enemies here."

Claire nodded. "So you keep my secret, you help me keep up the illusion, and I keep the others from getting back at you for some of the things you've done. That's the deal."

"Pretty much," J.D. said.

"And I'm just supposed to trust you?"

"You don't have much of a choice."

Claire hung her head. "All right. Deal. But no one gets hurt."

"Why would anyone get hurt?" J.D. asked.

Claire's gaze narrowed. "What is it you really want?"

J.D. laughed. It was a good question. One to which he was only starting to form an answer. "I'll have to get back to you on that one."

From down the shore, Bertram started calling.

"Gotta run," Claire said.

"Do you?"

She stopped. "Oh. Right."

"That's better," J.D. said. "Make him come to you. Let him know you'll do your part, but only 'cause you want to get out of here."

"Yeah," Claire said gruffly. "Why should he be runnin' the show? It's his fault we're back here."

"Now you got it," J.D. said. "You know, *Holly*, there might be hope for you yet."

He watched as she swayed in place to unseen music.

"I remember she used to do that," Claire said. "Holly."

"True enough."

After a couple of minutes, Bertram came over and commanded both "Holly" and J.D. to get back to work. There were trees that needed to be knocked down to build the litter that would carry the M.I.N.D. Machine. And there was gold to be found in the foothills.

A rumble sounded, and a cloud of gray ash shot into the sky from the top of the jagged volcano. Tiny flares of crimson spat within the cloud.

"It's starting," Bertram said. "I'd better go back to the others. Let them know that the flow won't begin for some time. The one thing we don't need is panic."

J.D. and Claire followed Bertram to the troops gathered on the shore. J.D. saw the awe all the others held for Bertram. He was their one shining hope.

No one saw things clearly. No one even wanted to consider that all this had happened because of one mistake after another that Bertram had made.

J.D. pictured what it would be like to have everyone looking at him that way—as if *he* were the guy with all the answers and *he* were the guy they'd follow without question.

What was it he really wanted? J.D. watched the crowd and grinned inwardly. Now he knew what he wanted—and just how to get it.

CHAPTER 10

AARON

Aaron had been working vine detail for hours. Bertram had assembled a collection of dinosaurs who had nice snapping beaks. They cut the vines into shorter lengths for other dinosaurs who walked on two legs and had some manual dexterity to twist together into ropes.

Jenny and Christine, two sisters who had landed in the bodies of chicken-sized Compsognathus, were expert cutters. They were also two of the best food gatherers for the meat-eating segment of the population. The compies moved in a blur, capturing little lizards and ratlike mammals, while Holly's scissorlike jaw had been incredibly useful in digging into warrens and dragging out prey.

Holly was also on tree-smashing detail, and she was acting a little scarier with every tree she took down.

"Fine," she muttered, advancing on a tree. "You want it that way? Fine!"

She surged at the tree and smashed it to pieces. Other dinosaurs ducked for cover behind rocks as shards of wood flew through the air.

Jenny and Christine scampered up to Aaron.

"Someone's got to talk to her," Jenny chirped.

"She's really losing it!" Christine added.

Aaron was hungry, cold, and tired. But everyone knew that he was Bertram's brother, and so they were looking at him as if he was second in command or something. He sighed and wondered how Colonel Charmin would handle things.

Of course, it was complicated, because he actually kind of liked Holly, though he felt guilty about that. After all, it was seeing Claire in Wetherford that had really woken him up from the daze he'd been in ever since the accident that killed his mother.

When he approached Holly, she had her head down and was building up a head of steam to go after another tree.

"Yo!" Aaron said. "Holly, can I talk to you?"

"Yeah, one second," she replied.

He darted for cover as she demolished another tree. She sauntered over to him when she was done.

"So what's up?" Holly asked.

He dusted splinters off his scaly hide and nodded to the huge mass of timber Holly had created. "Have you gone over and taken a look at the M.I.N.D. Machine?"

Holly shook her head.

"It's pretty big. What we're gonna need are lengths of wood that are a good twelve or fifteen feet."

Holly looked back to the timber and angled her head a little.

"I'm worried that what you're doing isn't working," Aaron said.

"Really?" Holly asked. Her nostrils flared.

For some reason Aaron didn't feel intimidated by Holly. He was totally comfortable in her presence. Maybe it was because they were both outsiders.

Aaron walked over to the timber with Holly. "I think what we need to do is bring down some of those bigger upper branches first, then saw through the base of some of these trees and bring down the trunks. Then we can polish the struts down like I did with my board. Would that work for you?"

"Oh," Holly said in a low, heated voice. "You're asking me, not telling me?"

A thunderous roar sounded in the distance. They turned to see more ash exploding into the sky. The temperature was dropping. Along the sides of several smaller volcanoes, fissures spat steam.

"Yeah, I'm asking," Aaron said.

"Um...all right. Fine," Holly said. "Show me what you're talking about."

From somewhere near, several small cries of relief

sounded. Dinosaurs slowly emerged from cover and got back to work.

Aaron led Holly deeper into the green forest. He thought about the things she'd been saying earlier before power-driving into the trees, and pointed to a ginkgo that was about forty-five feet high and leaning to the left. "I don't know about you, but I'm getting a bad feeling about that tree."

"Really?" Holly asked. "Why?"

Aaron shrugged. "Just...something about the way it's kind of not standing straight. Like it needs an attitude adjustment. A wake-up call."

A snort came from the predator beside Aaron. "I can see that."

"This whole grove here," Aaron said, pointing at a group of ginkgoes. The wedge-shaped foliage fluttered in the breeze. "I'd say they are *all* showing a notable lack of respect. Some examples must be made. A few of these guys should drop and give us twenty."

"Drop and give us twenty?" Holly asked.

"Army brat. Don't mind me," Aaron said. "Now, I'm thinking we could take some of the smaller chunks of wood you cut before, file down some stones, and make kind of an ax for you to swing. You could take these out quick and clean, then we could set to work on making the flooring for the litter we have to build."

"Think that up all on your own, huh?" Holly asked.

"Yeah, but don't let it get around—it'll ruin my image."

"I don't think your image is in any danger," Holly said. "But I've got another idea."

She walked over to the tree, hugged it, wrestled with it a little, then hauled it out of the ground, roots trailing. She let it fall to one side. "How's that?"

"Yeah," Aaron said. "That'll work."

In the distance, another cloud of ash blew from the sharp ridges of the volcano.

Aaron admired the beauty and majesty of the volcano, and suddenly realized that Bertram had forgotten something very important.

"Listen," Aaron said. "Can I trust you?"

"I don't know. Can you?"

"I think so. Do me a favor, okay? Let it rip on one of those lower branches. Just mash it up."

Holly lifted her little arms. "Sure."

She whacked the branch with the side of her face. It cracked and fell. She hesitated, looking to Aaron with a trace of shyness and embarrassment he never would have expected, then turned and stomped the branch. The old anger soon lit in her eyes, and she roared as she reduced the branch to kindling.

Aaron had to call to her five times before she stopped.

"Right," he said, picking up a splintered chunk of wood. He nodded at the spewing volcano. "We need to go up there. It's not a long climb. We can be back in an hour, and then we can really get into this."

Holly nodded. "Okay, I'm curious. Let's go."

They circled around the group and chose a path between the other work areas so that no one would notice their quick exit. The climb up the side of the volcano took only twenty minutes. Soon they were standing as close as they dared to the rim. Bits of rock flew upward and sailed down. A few came close to the spot Aaron had chosen.

"The thing is, there are rituals in every culture that are, like, supposed to keep the lava safely underground," Aaron said. "We used to live in Hawaii, and the native Hawaiians went and offered gifts to Pele, the fire goddess, who's supposed to live in one of the craters there. I'm thinking you're about as close to a fire goddess as we have. Explosive, powerful, brave, all that good stuff."

Aaron held out the chunk of wood to Holly. "So you should make the offering. It ought to buy us some time."

Holly took the offering and stared at it.

"I picked that one because the jagged edges are like the ones on this crater," Aaron said. "And because of what you put into it when you were bust-ing it up. I figure whatever's living in the volcano will like that."

"You really think this'll make a difference?" Holly asked.

"Maybe. Oh, and you can make a wish while you're at it."

Holly closed her eyes. Her jaw moved just a little. Aaron guessed she was making her wish, so he took the time to make his own.

"I wish Claire were here," he whispered.

A sudden roar came from his companion, and Aaron stumbled back as Holly tossed the wood high into the air. It struck one of the rocky uprises and bounced off, breaking into tiny little splinters as it made its way halfway down the volcano and vanished into the mist clinging to the lower reaches.

"Oops," Holly said coldly. "So much for our wishes, huh? And as far as the tree cutting is concerned, I can take it from here."

She turned so quickly she nearly knocked him over with her tail. Aaron leaped out of her way and watched her stomp down the path they had taken along the side of the volcano, wondering what had caused her sudden angry eruption.

CHAPTER 11

BERTRAM

Bertram was exhausted, and it was only the middle of the day.

For hours he had been going from one group of students to another, making sure that everyone was doing what they were supposed to be doing and not slacking off.

Getting the plant-gatherers to stockpile food and *not* eat it had been one of the most trying tasks. Bertram had taken that one on personally. After all, his first trip back in time had been in the body of an Ankylosaurus, so he could certainly understand their craving to do nothing but eat all the time.

Reggie seemed to have the fish-gatherers motivated with his music-and-D.J. routine. And when Bertram had last checked on Aaron's crew, it appeared they were getting plenty of vine cut and tied into strong rope, while Holly was taking care of the timber.

Finally Bertram returned to the group dealing with

the machine. Ash falling from the erupting volcano had half buried Bertram's creation. Now it needed to be dug out. J.D. and several others were working this detail, and the task was nearly complete.

"Hey, it's the boss man," J.D. said, sifting through the fine gray ash. He and all the other dinosaurs were covered with it.

Thunderclaps sounded from the volcano. Bertram watched as everyone but J.D. looked toward the jagged peak in fear.

"You really think the lava's not gonna come down sooner rather than later?" Melissa asked in a quavering voice. "I mean, how can you really know?"

"Because Will downloaded the data from the M.I.N.D. Machine," Bertram said. "His version of it, anyway."

She looked back and gave the side panel of the machine a solid kick. "It's all this thing's fault!"

Bertram was so surprised by Melissa's sudden outburst that he didn't know how to react. Instead, J.D. stomped over to her.

"Hey, that's not gonna help," he said. "Everything's gonna be all right. Bertram and the machine are gonna get us home. That's what you want, isn't it?"

Melissa lowered her head. "I want to go home right now."

"We all do," J.D. said. "That's why we're working

so hard for the boss man here. He's gonna get us back. Isn't that right, Bertram?"

Bertram nodded slowly, wishing he could make himself look more confident. "Yeah. You bet, we're getting out of this."

Melissa looked down at the panel she had dented. "Sorry."

The group quietly went back to work. After ten minutes J.D. looked over.

"So help me out, *Bertram*," J.D. said loudly. Very loudly. So loudly that all the surrounding dinosaurs turned to hear what was being said. "I'm trying to

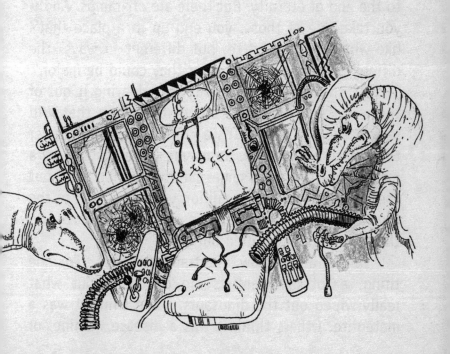

understand—that place we all saw, the Dinoverse, that's what our world becomes if we don't make it back, right?"

Bertram was a bit uneasy about the faces looking toward him for answers. On the other hand, he was happy J.D. had asked him about scientific theory. Science was something he could handle—something he *liked* to talk about—and that's what he focused on.

"Well, it's not necessarily what *our* world will become," he told J.D.

"Yeah? Why not?"

"Picture reality like a freeway stretching from here to the end of eternity. But there are off-ramps. And if you take one of those, you end up in a place that's like what you're used to, but different in ways. The differences could be subtle, or they could be major."

J.D. shoved at a mound of ash, clearing it out of the way. "Like that bite out of the moon that Will saw in the Dinoverse. It's a crater, isn't it? A crater that *isn't* in our moon. So maybe it was caused by a meteorite—the very same meteorite that took out the dinosaurs sixty-five million years ago. But in the Dinoverse, it hit the moon instead of the Earth. So the dinosaurs never died out."

"Well, I don't know," Bertram admitted. "For one thing, a lot of scientists are divided about what really wiped out the dinosaurs. Some think it was a meteorite. Others think it was a disease, famine, or any number of things. After all, a lot of smaller animals survived."

"There's something else I don't get," J.D. said. "In the Dinoverse, there were dinosaurs from all different time periods. I mean, I was into dinosaurs once. I know that you're not supposed to have a T. rex and a Stegosaurus at the same time. It doesn't really add up."

"That's why I think the Dinoverse is something else entirely," Bertram said. "The age of dinosaurs, the Mesozoic, was divided into three distinct periods: the Triassic, the Jurassic, and the Cretaceous. The reason for breaking it up is because there were three separate extinction events.

"Lots of dinosaurs were only around for short lengths of time," continued Bertram, "then they went away. In the Dinoverse, that didn't seem to have happened. So it can't be our reality."

"Except that they had a pretty good grasp of science," J.D. said. "Whatever they put their minds to, they could, like, *make* happen. DNA research and all could have been in their grasp. So they could have just brought those extinct dinos back. And another thing—look around you."

Bertram and J.D. looked at all the dinosaur faces staring at them.

"We're looking at that same thing, aren't we?" J.D. challenged. "I mean, we have all sorts of dinosaurs coexisting from different periods right here and now. So maybe things are already too far gone. I mean, the Dinoverse *could* be our reality after all. Our world could be changed forever. Human evolution swapped for a dinosaur civilization. In which case, we're actually in deep doo-doo, wouldn't you agree?"

Bertram's shoulders slumped. "Yes, that could be true. I can't disagree with that hypothesis. I can only hope it isn't true."

Footsteps came from behind, and Bertram turned to see Aaron approaching.

"We've got the wood. It's being smoothed down," Aaron said. "Shouldn't be long before we're ready."

"That's great," Bertram answered, but his mind was still focused on the possibilities J.D. had raised.

"You guys look like you're almost done," Aaron said, glancing at all the dinosaurs gathered around, listening.

"Just having a little talk to make the time go faster," Bertram said. "J.D. was mentioning the temporal anomalies we're looking at in this region."

"Oh?" Aaron said.

"No big thing," said J.D.

"But it is," Bertram said.

He noticed Aaron studying the faces of the students who had gathered around. "I think J.D.'s right," Aaron said uneasily. "No big thing."

"No, it *is*," Bertram said. "The M.I.N.D. Machine never does anything without a reason—"

"But—"

"No," continued Bertram. "I think I've figured out what happened. When Mr. London first activated the M.I.N.D. Machine, it wasn't just Will, Patience, and Zane who went back. There were dozens of other students thrown back to all parts of the Mesozoic, too.

"Mr. London told me that he had gone back and helped them all come home. He said he'd gone on many rescues. He just couldn't remember them because they were actions he still needed to take in his future. I know it's hard to follow—at the time I didn't believe him, either. But now I do, and—"

Aaron tried to interrupt. "Bertram, now's not the time to—"

But J.D. spat a grinding stone that struck Aaron in the shoulder. "Let him talk if he wants to!" J.D. cried.

Bertram ignored the exchange, because he didn't want to stop talking. He wanted to get it all out. "You see, I wanted the M.I.N.D. Machine taken apart so that this could never happen again. Mr. London turned it on, and I misunderstood what he was doing. I didn't believe he had another mission—to bring more students back to the present. I got in the middle of things to try to stop him. I pushed him out of the way, and then everything went crazy."

Suddenly Bertram felt a crushing guilt descend on

him. He looked at the other students. "It's all of you. *You* were the ones Mr. London was supposed to help find your way home. I kept him from going back to help you. And when I did that, you were all pulled here, to this *one* spot in time. That's why you're all here from different periods of the Mesozoic. It's *my* fault. All of this is my fault."

With those final words, J.D.'s head bobbed with a kind of glee.

But Bertram didn't have time to consider why J.D. seemed so happy, as footfalls suddenly sounded from a nearby crest.

Bertram looked beyond the group of dark, accusing faces gathered around him and saw a Stygimoloch running his way.

"The scissor-jaws are back!" the dinosaur said. "They're back, and they're going after everyone!"

CHAPTER 12

J.D.

J.D. ran with the others, thrilled at what he'd accomplished. He'd actually gotten Bertram to admit that this was all *his* fault, that everyone would have been safe at home if not for him.

It was perfect.

The only real problem was Aaron. Clearly Aaron could tell that Bertram was being played. Something would have to be done about him. J.D. didn't know what, but he was certain that, as Will had said, everything happens for a reason, and that an opportunity would present itself.

They reached the shore. Claire was front and center with the spike-tails, growling and snapping.

She was turning in a pretty good performance as Holly Cronk. J.D. never could have pictured Crystal Claire facing off against predators like this.

Or maybe there was more to Claire than even she knew about. If that was the case, he could use it to his advantage, too.

J.D. saw what had attracted the scissor-jaws. The vast mound of fish Reggie and his crew had caught was piled up on the shoreline. *What a smell!*

Now good old Reggie the hardheaded pachy was quivering among a patch of trees a few hundred yards back.

"We've got to find some way to let them know not to come back!" Bertram hollered. "This place won't be safe for them by tomorrow."

J.D. saw Aaron glance at Bertram, then at him. Aaron looked incredulous. Obviously the guy understood the mistakes Bertram was making, but Bertram was oblivious.

As the leader, Bertram had everyone's awe and respect, but he was making his decisions based on logic alone. He wasn't stopping to consider the emotional state of the other students.

Sure, they were scared and they wanted the scissor-jaws gone. But none of them wanted to get wounded or eaten in some full-fledged battle!

A soft cry came from the treeline. J.D. took another look at Reggie and saw the odd way he was cradling his shoulder. It looked as though someone had already gotten hurt.

"They're hungry," J.D. said. "If we feed them, give 'em *some* of our fish, they won't have any reason to hassle us. Or to try to eat any of us."

Bertram and Aaron stopped.

"No one asked you," Aaron said.

"He's right," Bertram said. "If we fight, who knows what might happen."

Bertram gestured to the spike-tails. "Go over to the fish, split the catch in half, then make three piles out of one of the halves. Leave the piles where they can reach them, but guard the rest."

"No way!" Aaron said. "We worked hard to get all that food, and we're gonna need it after the lava flow cuts off the way to the beach. Those guys can go down to the shore and do their own fishing!"

"Do it," Bertram said firmly. "J.D.'s right. They're not smart like us. They can't think things out like that. They'll just keep coming back and attacking."

J.D. wanted to laugh. He pictured the version of himself that he had seen in the Dinoverse. The idea of that other self had angered him. It was so much like his gentle, soft, stupid father. But now he was seeing that there was strength in intelligence and cunning. And reason could be wielded with the same explosive force as an unexpected fist to the face.

The spike-tails looked over at Bertram. One of them angled his head in J.D.'s direction. "We're taking orders from *him* now? Do you know what he used to do to us? Do you know what kind of—"

"It's a good idea," Bertram said firmly. "Do it."

The spike-tails shook their heads but cautiously

divided up the fish. One of the scissor-jaws rushed forward, but Claire met it, roaring so loudly that even the advancing scissor-jaw jumped and drew back.

Soon the fish had been divided up. Claire and the spike-tails gave the predators room to reach the three piles of fish. Two of the big predators collided and scrapped for a time over the closest pile while the third munched down on the farthest batch over.

When the third one finished and moved toward the next pile, the other two shoved it back and devoured all that had been set out for them.

Finally all three scissor-jaws moved toward the food that the Wetherford gang was saving for themselves. This was the moment of truth.

"You're on," whispered J.D.

Claire stepped up, glared at them with fury, and roared her head off. That was all it took for the three scissor-jaws to back off. They'd had their meal, and their bellies were full—they were in too good a mood for a fight now.

The three predators loped away happily, vanishing down the winding coastline in less than a minute. The Wetherford group just stood there, their mouths hanging open at the retreating predators.

"Okay," one of the spike-tails finally said. "Maybe it was a good idea after all."

J.D. stood back and watched as Aaron took

Bertram off to the side and began a heated conversation with him. He couldn't hear what they were saying, but from the way they both kept looking his way, it wasn't hard to guess.

He heard loud stomps and looked up as Claire's shadow fell on him.

She waited a long time, then spoke. "I'm impressed."

J.D. couldn't remember the last time he'd received a compliment. He couldn't think of anything to say except, "You weren't so bad yourself."

Claire's head bobbed. "I think I've figured out what you want," she said.

J.D. tensed. "Really?"

She nodded. "Yeah. Forget about me looking out for you. What if we could set it up so there wasn't any need?"

"I'm listening," J.D. said. He started to relax. She didn't have a clue what he was really up to.

"Reggie's hurt."

"Yeah. Someone's got a boo-boo. What's it to me?"

"Your father's a doctor, right?"

"So?"

"So you know how to deal with stuff like this, don't you?" Claire asked.

"Maybe."

"Listen, I'm on to you, J.D. You're not so different from me. You want to change your image. You want people to look at you like maybe you're a real human being."

They were silent for a moment, staring at each other's dinosaur bodies.

"You know what I mean," Claire said.

He knew *exactly* what she meant. Just like most of the people he knew, she was making an assumption that what *she* wanted was the same thing everyone else wanted. But that was rarely the case.

Still, raising his profile did fit into his overall agenda. "We'd need help to fix him. How about your buddy Aaron?"

"Does it have to be him?"

J.D. was surprised by that. Maybe things weren't so great between the two of them after all. "Bertram should be focusing on getting everyone back to work, and we could use someone with hands, like a Dilophosaurus. And everyone likes Aaron. They'll listen to him."

A sour puff of air escaped her nostrils as she sighed. "All right, I'll get him."

Soon Bertram was reorganizing the work details, and J.D. stood with Claire, Aaron, and the wounded Reggie.

"I gave old Ugly as good as I got," Reggie said. He cradled his arm as if it were a newborn kitten. "But those scissor-jaws were just too big."

"What do you want me to do?" Aaron asked.

J.D. angled his head from one side to the other, getting a little crick in his long neck as he studied Reggie's shoulder and arm.

"His arm looks okay," J.D. said. "Feel around his shoulder."

Aaron clamped his hands on Reggie's shoulder, and the hardhead howled in pain.

"*Gently* feel around his shoulder," J.D. said. "Describe how it feels."

Aaron approached Reggie again, but the pachy backed off. "It's not so bad."

"Come on," Claire said. "How are you gonna stand up for Melissa, or Claire when you get back home, if you don't get this taken care of? And keep the noise down. You've got an image."

"Oh," Reggie said. He straightened his back and held out his arm. "Oh, right!"

Aaron felt around and described everything.

"It's dislocated," J.D. said. He told Aaron exactly where and how to hold Reggie's arm and shoulder, then how much pressure would be needed to pop the end of the bone back into the socket. Reggie was given a small tree branch to bite down on. Even with the branch in his mouth, he wailed as Aaron manipulated his shoulder. Finally, there was a high, sharp pop, then it was finished. Reggie started to raise his arm and flinched.

"Just rest it for a while," J.D. said. "And be thankful nothing was broken."

"It doesn't hurt anymore," Reggie said. He looked at J.D. "How'd you do that? That was amazing."

He rushed off to a crowd of dinosaurs down the shore.

"I've got stuff to do," Aaron said. He wouldn't look at J.D.

"Hey, Aaron," J.D. said. "You know how things will be when we get back?"

Aaron nodded.

"I don't want to get kicked out of school," J.D. said. "I don't care what my dad would think, or pretty much anyone else, but it would kill my mom. She wouldn't be able to take it, and I don't want her going through any more than she already has. Can you help me out?"

Aaron appeared stunned. "I—yeah. I—uh—understand about the mom stuff. Don't sweat it, okay? I'll tell 'em what I did. They'll probably let me off with a warning and stuff. Some detention, working around the school."

"I appreciate it," J.D. said. "I really do."

Aaron walked off.

Claire turned to J.D. "Now I'm *truly* impressed."

"Things change," J.D. told her. "People change. Being back here has given me time to think about what I really want. And I don't think I want to be Judgment Day Harms anymore."

He whacked her shoulder with the side of his head. "I'll leave all the heavy-duty work for you. Sound good?"

Before Claire could reply, Bertram started calling from the shore. Soon everyone was gathered around him.

"We've got four people missing!" Bertram said excitedly. "Jenny and Christine, who are compies, Marv, a sixth-grader who's a Hypsilophodon, and Joey, a seventh-grader in the body of a Lesothosaurus. The compies look like chickens, the others like salamanders or frogs—"

"I saw them running off when the scissor-jaws came back!" exclaimed Melissa.

"Right," said Bertram. "I think their dino instincts took over and made them flee. We have to get them back. Holly, obviously you can take care of yourself, so I want you to find them and bring them back. The rest of us will keep working."

"Waitaminute," Claire said. "How am I supposed to find them?"

"Just pick up their scent," Bertram said. "It shouldn't be a big deal."

"But I'm not very good at the scent thing," said Claire, "and—"

J.D. cleared his throat. "Um, boss man?"

Bertram looked over. "I'm *not* the boss, J.D. I'm just trying to help us get home."

"Sure," J.D. said. "Listen, they were already scared off by the scissor-jaws. You send Holly and all they're gonna see and smell is another scissor-jaw. How about if Aaron goes with her?"

Claire and Aaron spun on him. "What?"

"You heard me," said J.D. "Aaron should really go with Holly. He can help Holly with the scent thing, and he can be the one to approach the runaways."

"I don't think—" Aaron began, but Bertram cut him off.

"It makes sense," Bertram said. "Aaron can convince them to come back, while Holly can make sure the other scissor-jaws don't serve up our little runaways as dessert."

"Perfect," Claire grumbled.

"Right. Thanks," Aaron said, glaring at J.D.

J.D. did his best to look earnest. "Hey, I'm just trying to do my part."

Inside, J.D. felt a happiness unlike any he had ever felt before. His plan was working.

By tonight he would have everything he wanted.

CHAPTER 13

CLAIRE

Claire and Aaron traveled through the foothills for hours. Aaron had the scent of the frightened foursome. Claire hadn't been able to pick up their trail at all. Fortunately the small group had stayed together.

She looked over to Aaron, who was totally focused on their mission. Her mind was a muddle. She resented his presence, but at the same time she was glad that she hadn't been sent off alone.

She studied Aaron. He was so comfortable in his new body. She lumbered around, always having to remind herself to keep her tail up off the ground, while he flowed gracefully up over rocks and through narrow passages.

"I've still got them," Aaron said. "They were pretty scared, so their scent was strong. I feel bad for them."

"Me too," Claire admitted.

They traveled for miles through twisting canyons. One of the tallest volcanoes had a sparkling river running down its left flank, all the way to the ocean.

"Clouds deposit rainwater on the mountain," Aaron said. "That's where all the water comes from."

Claire nodded. It was staggering to stand at the base of a rock so tall it literally disappeared into the clouds. It was late in the afternoon, and the sun was still bright. Despite that, the temperature was dropping and the daylight was straining to break through the ash hanging in the sky.

"We need to find them before it gets dark," Claire said.

They came to the edge of the river and saw that it made a sharp descent into a low valley, then continued along a snaking path into the distant mist.

Aaron sniffed the air. "We've been moving up. The elevation's been rising, but so gradually that we didn't even notice it."

Claire pointed at the churning water. "At least we know they're on this side. There's no way they could have crossed that thing. The current is too rapid."

"They went down there," Aaron said. He pointed at the base of the valley. "Not a rough climb down for little animals, but it's gonna be a bear for us."

An idea came to Claire. "That depends."

"Really?"

She looked down at him. He was only a third of her size, but his body was tough. "Ever do a cannonball?"

"In the pool, sure, but—"

Claire took a few steps back, then ran ahead and vaulted over a collection of flat stones overlooking the sharply falling river. Suddenly she was in the air, the deep water of the river's base far below.

"Yahhhhhhhh!" she hollered. She tucked her body in as best she could and held her breath as the churning flow rose up to grab her.

She hit the surface with the jolting force of a

three-story-high boulder tossed into the water and sank quickly below the waterline. Then she kicked and paddled to the surface, fought the flow, and made it to shore.

There. No arduous climb down for her. She shook herself off and looked up at Aaron.

He was slowly, carefully climbing down.

"Don't be a wuss!" she called. "Jump!"

Raising a claw, he waved and shook his head. She sat down and waited for him to reach her, chuckling a little as she remembered how she thought *he* was adventurous.

"Hey!" he yelled.

She looked up just in time to see him run from a lower shelf on the mountainside and leap into the air. He cannonballed into the river, splashing down like a bowling ball.

She laughed as his head burst from the water, and turned and offered her tail. When he grabbed on, she walked forward, dragging him to the shore. Soon they were both on the river's edge, panting and laughing.

"I bet *that's* not something you'd be doing with good old Crystal Claire," she said.

Aaron's laughter drifted away and an uncomfortable silence filled the air.

"Sorry," Claire said.

Just tell him, she thought. *He likes you, so go on, what's the big deal?*

"I guess that wasn't very cool of me, up by the volcano," Aaron said. "I'm sorry."

"No, it's my problem," she said. "I guess I was just a little jealous. No one's ever made a wish like that for me."

What are you talking about, you idiot? she thought. *It WAS for you!*

No, it was for someone he saw for two seconds and formed a whole opinion about, someone he's never even talked to, someone he doesn't have the first clue about.

"It's crazy," Aaron said. "but...have you ever felt like you've been sleepwalking, just going through life in a haze, then something happens and *bam*—you're wide awake? You have this moment of clarity, and that's when you know you were dreaming all the rest of the time. Only you didn't realize it before."

"Maybe," Claire said.

Aaron sniffed and pointed west. Claire rose with him, and they continued to track the missing students.

"That's what it was like for me when I heard Claire laughing," Aaron said.

"When you *heard* her?" Claire said. "Not when you saw her?"

Aaron shook his head. "She's beautiful, but so what?"

"Been there, done that, is that it?" Claire asked. "You stud."

Aaron laughed. "No. Well, a little. Enough to

know that the ones who care too much about the outside forget to think about the inside being mean or selfish or whatever. You know, you've got a pretty laugh, too. A lot like Claire's."

Nodding, Claire started walking. "We'd better get going. Quiet time's over."

"You bet."

They walked along the riverbank, then Aaron led them into a forest and to the foothills of more mountains. Claire wondered how many of them were volcanic. *All of them, probably,* she thought. *Just waiting for what's inside them to explode.*

She could relate.

Following Aaron, she thought about how comfortable it felt to be led by him. In fact, she had allowed herself to be led all her life by one person or another.

Oh, will you stop already? her agent cried in her mind. *You've done all the homework you need to do on playing the part of Crystal Claire. I swear, that's the one thing you need to work on: overanalyzing. For once, take a risk. Follow your gut.*

Claire stopped suddenly. She and Aaron had come to a junction leading to a narrow path that wound in two separate directions. Aaron had already gone off on the left-hand route.

"Aaron," Claire said, "you go that way. I'm gonna head in the other direction, see if we can find them any faster if we split up."

He nodded slowly, though he looked deep in thought. She waited for the objection. The warning that he had to stay and protect her, that she could get lost or hurt or—

"Yeah, good idea," Aaron said. "Their scent is all over this area. I think they've been scurrying back and forth for a while. Just let out a really good roar when you find 'em."

He turned and walked away. Claire watched him, her jaw hanging open. Then he turned a corner and vanished behind a hill.

He trusted her. Just like that.

Okay, she thought. *I'm not gonna overanalyze. I'm just gonna go with it.*

She went the other way, climbing along a steadily rising path that forked several times and led her through gray hills dotted with ash-covered trees.

It was getting darker now, and pretty soon it would be tough to find the way back. That is, it would be for a person. What about a dinosaur? Could she trust her instincts to lead her back when the time came?

"You're doing it again!" she yelled. A nasty roar left her throat.

A sudden scurrying sounded off to her left. She turned her head and saw motion. A pair of turkey-sized dinosaurs went zipping under a rocky overhang.

"Guys!" Claire shouted. "Guys, it's me, it's Cl—" She stopped herself. "It's Holly!"

Remaining perfectly still, Claire waited until the scurrying started up again. Two figures darted out and stopped before her on the path.

"We got lost," Jenny said.

Her companion nodded quickly. "Don't be mad."

"It's all right," Claire said. "We just need to get back to the group. Bertram's got a safe place picked out, and he should have them hauling the machine by now. And J.D. came up with a plan to keep the scissor-jaws from bothering us anymore."

Claire looked around. "Where are the other two?"

Jenny clucked. Christine echoed the sentiment.

"I've got something to tell you, but you're not going to like it," Jenny said.

"They're all right, aren't they?" Claire asked.

"Oh, they're fine," Christine said. "But they told us that no matter what, they're not going back."

CHAPTER 14

CLAIRE

Claire did her best to stay patient and calm as she followed the quickly moving little compies over a series of rises. If it became too dark to guide the runaways back today, she would make camp with them and take them back tomorrow.

No big deal.

"It's getting chilly," Claire said.

"That's why Marv and Joey picked the lake," Christine said. "It stays warm over there."

They topped a final rise, and Claire found herself looking down on a small lake ringed by ash-encrusted stones. The lake was about fifteen hundred feet across and nearly a perfect circle. It also bubbled and steamed like hot soup.

The Hypsilophodon and the Lesothosaurus sat on stones with their little feet hanging over the water. They turned quickly as Claire and the girls tromped over to them.

"Oh, thanks a lot!" the hippie said. "You couldn't

153

just say you didn't see which way we went, could you?"

"Nope," Christine said.

Claire came closer to the lake. "What is this?"

The froggy-looking Lesothosaurus raised his snout. "The whole lake is filled with a corrosive. Like battery acid. Nice and warm, though. Toasty!"

"Yeah, just don't slip," Marv said. He whacked his buddy with his tail. Joey yelped as he nearly lost his balance, then leaped off the stones to the shore. Marv fell on his butt laughing.

"That wasn't funny!" Joey hollered.

"It was from here," Marv said.

"Look, guys," Claire said, "there's still some light in the sky. Let's head back."

"Here it comes," Jenny said.

Marv stood up. "Go back and do what? Get bossed around some more? Get eaten? No way."

"Told you," Christine murmured.

Claire frowned inwardly. "No one's going to eat you."

"Tell that to the other three big uglies your size. We're safe here. The vegetation's all ruined, so no plant-eaters will be around, and without plant-eaters to munch on, the predators won't come. It's simple."

"Well, that's great," Claire said. "And what do you guys eat?"

Marv waved his little claws in the air. "We're working on that."

"Yeah!" Joey said. "The important thing is choice. Free will! And—"

A roar sounded from the opposite crest. All of the smaller dinosaurs froze. Claire didn't worry. She assumed it was Aaron looking for her.

She answered the roar.

"No!" Marv yelped. "What are you doing?"

Claire realized her mistake a moment too late. Not one, but three forms topped the rise at the other side of the lake.

The scissor-jaws.

"They must like that it's warm here, too," Joey said. He shuddered as he spoke.

The predators raced down the ridge, one of them tripping and stumbling in his excitement.

"Stay calm," Claire said, her heart thundering. "And stay together."

All four smaller dinosaurs wailed in fear and ran in opposite directions.

"I said *stay CALM!*" Claire roared.

The little dinosaurs froze in their tracks and looked her way, their eyes wide with terror. Claire didn't know exactly where her outburst had come from. She wasn't *in* character anymore—she had *become* her character. This wasn't playtime. If she made a mistake, at least one if not all of her companions would end up on the scissor-jaws' menu.

She watched the advancing trio and said, "Joey, you've been all over this area, right?"

"Uh-huh," Joey squeaked.

"Were there any areas your gut instinct told you to avoid at all cost?" Claire asked. "Even if you didn't see any real problem?"

"Plenty."

"Get us to the worst of them."

Joey ran off, the other three small dinosaurs following. Claire trailed them to the top of a rise, stopping only to uproot a thirty-foot tree.

The trio of scissor-jaws was racing upward just behind them, and Claire kicked the tree down at them. It rolled on its side, its brittle branches snapping off. Two of the scissor-jaws got their legs tangled by it and tripped, falling to the foot of the rise. The tree sailed off past them, splashing into the corrosive lake. The scissor-jaws who had fallen nearby were splashed by the scalding waters, and they hollered in surprise and pain.

The third scissor-jaw came right for Claire.

I am not a thirteen-year-old girl, Claire hollered in her mind. *I am a dinosaur, I am a predator, and I am not afraid of letting you know how I feel, buddy!*

The scissor-jaw's maw opened as its bulk rushed at Claire. She stooped, grabbed a fallen branch, and smacked the dinosaur in the face. Teeth cracked and flew, and the dinosaur's head snapped back. Its little arms pinwheeled, and it fell down the hill.

Claire turned, not waiting to see the big, ugly thing land or to see if its friends were getting up or if they had had enough. She saw the scurrying forms of the runaway dinosaurs along the main path, barely visible in the gathering dusk, and raced after them.

It wasn't long before she heard thunderous footfalls behind them.

The little dinos raced for higher ground. Claire saw dozens of little niches and hiding places they might have chosen, but they continued on in a blur.

Climbing wasn't nearly so easy for Claire, and that meant it wasn't easy for their pursuers, either. She leaped from one ledge to another along the side of the mountain. Her vast bulk was almost too wide for the narrow shelves of rock that had been carved by erosion and other forces of nature.

Grunts and roars of complaint came from behind her.

"Come on, just give up," Claire growled. But when she looked over her shoulder, she saw the other scissor-jaws rapidly moving up the mountain.

She looked around and spotted a handful of boulders. Without glancing back, Claire kicked and tossed the rocks down behind her. The predators roared and wailed as the stones fell toward them.

Claire heard thuds and skittering sounds. She climbed higher, kicking down as many rocks as she could. The top of the mountain loomed. She coiled her muscles and sprang upward.

Clearing the crest of the mountain, Claire landed on a wide plateau covered in a drifting blue-white mist. The small group of runaways huddled a hundred yards away. *Why did they stop?* she wondered. *Why—*

At that instant, a geyser of scalding water erupted from a crack in the earth a half dozen feet in front of her!

Claire raced out of the way as the boiling water advanced across the hard, flat surface of the mountaintop like the claws of a deadly predator.

"Don't move!" Claire cried to her companions. "Stay calm, stay—"

Another geyser erupted, this one midway between Claire and the group. It sent steam and boiling water fifty feet into the air and hissed with a terrifying ferocity. A wall of steam and mist kept her from seeing if the others were all right.

When it finally cleared, her fellow students were nowhere to be seen.

"No," Claire whispered.

Behind her, she heard the first of the other scissor-jaws cautiously climbing the mountain again. She didn't bother turning. Bertram had made it all very clear: Either they *all* went back, or *no one* went back.

Jenny, Christine, Marv, and Joey...they were gone. Taken in a blink by this heartless land.

Her land now. Her time. Her home.

Footsteps came closer, began to surround her.

"I told them to come here," she whispered to herself. "I figured somehow I could keep them safe."

The footfalls grew louder. Low, unhappy growls sounded from her left, her right, and directly behind her.

"I told them to ignore their instincts," she said. "All because of the three of you."

She turned slowly, taking in the sight of three crouching, angry scissor-jaws.

"You want me?" she asked. "Come and get me."

Turning, she bolted across the plateau. From a fissure to her left, a sudden explosion of vapor lifted her off her feet and sent a burning, stinging rain against her skin.

Claire tumbled to the ground, listening for the roars of her attackers over the hiss of the geyser. She couldn't hear a thing. But she felt the heavy thumps of their huge feet as they came her way, their fury blinding them to the danger.

Claire got to her feet and ran. She roared defiantly, letting them know exactly where she was. A geyser went off before her, and she circled around it. Another exploded a hundred feet to her left.

Then she felt something else. It wasn't a physical thing. The earth didn't tremble. The boiling rains didn't fall upon her.

Instead, she suddenly *knew* just where the next geyser would erupt. She sensed it. Felt its mounting tension and excitement, as if it truly were a living thing.

What she felt made no sense. It was an instinct. She followed it.

"Come on, guys," Claire said. She positioned herself as best she could, crouching low as if she were ready to confront the predators claw to claw.

The scissor-jaws raced at her, and she did her best to give them a wide smile of welcome.

Suddenly, just as the biggest of the three closed on her, a geyser erupted from a fissure just beneath his feet. The blast of steam lifted him a dozen feet into the air and sent his squealing form hissing back into a huge wall of mist. Claire stood still as the boiling water fell, soaking the other two scissor-jaws and missing her by inches.

The predators fell to their sides, their scales burned away, steam rising from their quaking bodies.

Claire turned her back on them in contempt and walked deeper into the mist floating across the mountaintop. It was disarmingly beautiful. The sense she'd possessed of when and where the next geyser would blow had left her. She knew that at any moment what had happened to the other scissor-jaws and to the runaways she had tried to protect might happen to her.

But it didn't. She heard the geysers erupt behind her and off to either side. She had a sense that one went off in the exact area she had just left, a geyser that might have taken her had she remained.

She just kept walking.

Then a new instinct overtook her. Her nostrils flared, and she smelled fear and relief—along with the rich smell of prey.

"Jenny?" she asked.

A tiny little reptile stepped out from behind a huge boulder just ahead. She was followed by three others.

The runaways! They were all right!

Claire sank to her knees in relief.

"That was incredible!" Marv yelled.

"Yeah!" Joey said. "You just tell us what to do, and we'll do it. We were crazy not to trust you guys."

Footfalls sounded from behind the group. Christine yelped as Aaron appeared.

"Hey, there you are," he said. "Did I miss anything?"

Marv and Joey rushed to Aaron. They related all that Claire had done—so quickly that Aaron had to laugh and tell them to slow down a half dozen times.

Aaron. Claire shook her head. She hadn't even *thought* of Aaron. The idea of someone coming to her rescue hadn't even occurred to her.

Listening to the compies and the others tell Aaron about all she had done gave Claire a sense of pride and power that she had never before felt. She was changing her image from the inside out, and that felt better than anything!

For a moment she wondered if J.D. felt like this now that he seemed to be changing for the better, too—

Suddenly Claire stopped. Her heart sank as she suspected something about J.D.

She recalled how strongly he'd insisted that Aaron go with her on this mission. Yet she hadn't needed Aaron at all.

Claire had stupidly assumed J.D. was acting like so many other guys before him, wanting to protect Crystal Claire by sending someone else along with her.

But that wasn't why he'd wanted Aaron to go.

"We've got to get back," Claire said. "Something is going to happen. I know it. I can feel it."

"What?" Aaron asked. "Holly, what—"

She looked for a way off the plateau. "Come on, Aaron. We've got to get back *now*!"

CHAPTER 15

J.D.

J.D. Harms was about to have the best night of his life. He couldn't wait for it to begin!

Just after Claire and Aaron had left, the other dinosaurs had finished assembling the litter to carry the M.I.N.D. Machine. Workers had moved the damaged machine as carefully as they could. But one of the young students, who still wasn't used to his saurian strength, had broken a control panel while setting it down on the litter

Bertram had been furious, and ever since he'd been treating that helper as if he were an idiot.

J.D. *loved* it.

Now, despite the descending darkness and the complaints of the other students, Bertram was still pushing everyone hard. Dragging the litter over the rough terrain was very difficult and went very slowly. It gave many of the dinosaurs time to talk.

"It's all Bertram's fault," a pair whispered back and forth. "He even said it was! We heard him!"

"He doesn't even know if this is going to work," one complained to another. "We could go through all this and still be stuck here."

"And I thought he was so cool..."

As the twilight deepened into evening, crews were rotated and food breaks were allowed. But every time they stopped, Bertram paced anxiously and muttered about how little time they had, how precious it was, and how he couldn't believe that no one but him got what was happening.

And people listened.

The spike-tails were the two main haulers. They took shifts with a wide harness that had been made to allow them to pull the litter. J.D. gave each of them a break for a stretch, and one of them apologized for the way they had treated him earlier.

"I needed a wake-up call," J.D. told them with as much sincerity as he could muster. "No hard feelings."

Inside he was already making future plans for each of them.

When nightfall came, everyone thought they would stop. But Bertram taught several of the students how to make torches, and they continued by firelight.

"Bad things can happen if we stop now," Bertram explained. "We can rest once we've got the machine in a safe place."

Far into the night they continued to labor. The

spike-tails were still hauling the litter while others were bringing food and supplies up the tall mountain with quivering legs.

Bertram helped out, and that was good. It meant he wasn't paying attention to J.D.

"Time for me to take a turn," J.D. said. The spike-tail who had been hauling the machine nodded with appreciation. They were halfway up the mountain, and the terrain was getting rougher all the time.

J.D. looked at the heavily knotted vines that served as carry ropes. The last two times he had taken a turn hauling the machine, he had used the sharp claws on his front paws to wear away part of those vines. He was able to spot the worn areas at once. The strain of pulling the heavy machine had thinned them out even more.

J.D. made sure no one was looking, then slashed at the vines some more before he slipped his head through the harness and allowed it to slide down his long neck to his blubbery torso.

He hauled the machine for half an hour without complaint, though his legs were buckling and his breath was strained. The harness hadn't been made for him, and it hurt like crazy. But all the effort and the pain would be worth it in the end.

When J.D.'s turn was over, one of the spike-tails had two helpers put the harness on him. Then he started trudging up the incline again.

J.D. sensed that it would happen soon, so he went over to Bertram.

"I think everyone could use a little sleep," J.D. said. "Will said we had time."

"I know," Bertram said. "But what if the information *his* M.I.N.D. Machine was accessing related to the past of *that* world, not *this* one?"

"The Dinoverse?" J.D. asked. "So you really don't think the Dinoverse and our future are one and the same?"

"The only way they're the same is if we fail," Bertram said. "And unfortunately, I'm all too aware of that possibility. Hope for the best, plan for the worst— that's what Mr. London would say if he were here."

He'd also be watching your back, J.D. thought. *Too bad for you, pal.*

Suddenly there was a loud snap like the cracking of a whip. Screams filled the night. J.D. and Bertram looked up to see the spike-tails who had been hauling the machine slipping down the mountainside, the litter crashing and bouncing as it fell, too.

One of the two lines attaching the harness had snapped, and the other was pulled taut. The spike-tail who was still attached to the litter dug in his feet and kept himself from being dragged down any farther, but the harness was pulled tight around his neck.

"Get it off me!" the spike-tail screamed. "It's choking me!"

"Wait!" Bertram yelled.

He was too late. A student in the body of a Microvenator flashed his razor-sharp claws and severed the other vine rope.

Then the litter bearing the M.I.N.D. Machine slipped away, bouncing and flying end over end into the mist at the base of the mountain.

They never heard it crash.

Every last dinosaur stood in silence and stared at the dark abyss below them.

"No," Bertram whispered in shock. "This can't be happening. It can't..."

J.D. stepped away from Bertram and went to the spike-tail who had been choked by the harness.

"Get this off him!" J.D. commanded, nodding toward the harness. Reggie and several other dinosaurs were there in seconds, helping to remove the harness.

Bertram stood alone, continuing to stare down into the darkness. "We've got to get down there. We've got to see how bad the damage is, then get to work on building another harness!"

J.D. shook his head. He had thought for most of the afternoon about just the right way to play this moment. Shouting at Bertram wasn't the way to go. It might just make some of the others feel sorry for him. Instead, J.D. put on his most sorrowful voice.

"Bertram, it's over," J.D. said.

The Dilophosaurus shook his head. "No. We can't give up. We'll never get back."

"We're *not* getting back," J.D. said. "I think most of us knew that the second we saw what had happened to the machine. But none of us had the heart to say it."

J.D. heard weeping. He looked over and saw Melissa. She had reacted not only the way he had expected her to react, but perfectly on cue.

"I'm sorry," J.D. said. "I don't like saying this. But someone has to."

Fred and his fellow Stegosaurus slammed their tails angrily on the ground.

"Tell him!" Fred hollered. "Tell him what we're all thinking!"

"You're not in charge of this thing anymore," J.D. said to the quaking, incredulous Dilophosaurus. "You're not in charge of *us* anymore. We can't help the future. But we can try to help ourselves."

J.D. turned his back on Bertram. "If it's okay with everyone, just for a while, I'll try to help us get through. And I'll try to come up with a plan that will take care of each and every one of you."

"What are you saying?" Bertram challenged. "What plan? There's only one plan. We've got to hope the machine can be fixed. That we can get it to safety in time and get it working."

"Hope is the enemy," J.D. said. "I'm sorry, but it is. Hope will have us putting our lives on the line for nothing. But if we face reality, if we look at things the way they really are, then I know we can get through." J.D. raised his head high. "If you're with me, just say my name."

"J.D.," Reggie said.

"J.D.!" Fred echoed.

Then the name became a chant, a powerful cry that was nearly as loud as the rumble of the volcano in the distance.

J.D. looked at the shattered little dinosaur who

had commanded so much loyalty and respect just a short time ago. With his tail drooping, Bertram walked away.

Just then flames spiraled from the jagged volcano. To J.D., they looked like fireworks. A celebration. He had won. The night was his!

And soon the future would be his as well.

To be continued in
DINOSAURS ATE MY HOMEWORK

HERE'S A SNEAK PEEK AT

#6

DINOSAURS ATE
MY HOMEWORK

by Scott Ciencin

Aaron couldn't believe what had just happened. The darkness had swallowed him whole, and suddenly he was standing in the gym of Wetherford Junior High.

Aaron looked down and saw scales, claws, and brilliant flashes of color across his Dilophosaurus body.

Was he dreaming? Had he fallen and hit his head?

Just one minute before, he had been in the past, surrounded by the rough terrain of prehistoric southern California, the sky above streaked with the crimson glow from erupting volcanoes.

He remembered running full speed away from

J.D.'s dinosaur posse. He'd run right toward a pitch-black opening, thinking it was some sort of cave.

Now he knew it wasn't a cave.

When he'd turned around, a swirling black space was all he could see, and Aaron realized he'd crossed into a vortex. He'd found some sort of *door* between the past and the present! Only—he was still a dinosaur!

Suddenly, blinding light filled the gym. Someone had switched on the lights, and Aaron saw that he wasn't alone. Dozens of dinosaurs stood about him, circling him warily. Others sat on the bleachers, looking on with gnashing teeth and clicking claws as a trio of raptors approached.

"You shouldn't be here," the first raptor said. "And that door behind you can't be allowed to exist. Not if we're going to get what we want."

Who are they? Aaron wondered.

The raptors crouched, looking as if they were going to spring at any moment. He heard tearing sounds. With a downward glance, he registered that he and the raptors were standing on a huge wrestling mat, their claws cutting into it.

"Enough talk," the first raptor said. He looked to his friends. "You guys know what needs to be done."

Aaron tried to prepare himself for the attack. There was no way out of this. He'd have to stand and fight.

No more excuses, Aaron thought. *Bummer, 'cause*

I'd really like to use the one about dinosaurs eating my homework!

Then the raptors were on him, and they were quicker than he could have believed. They leaped at him, claws and maws flashing.

The next thing he knew, it was wrestling-raptor mania!

#6

DINOSAURS ATE MY HOMEWORK

COMING IN NOVEMBER 2000

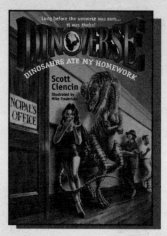

#6

DINOSAURS ATE MY HOMEWORK
by Scott Ciencin

"I'M OUT OF EXCUSES AND *WAY* OUT OF TIME!"

My name is Aaron Aimes. I've been sent to the principal's office more times than I can count. And I've had excuses for everything from gym to homework. No one's ever expected much from me. But it's hard to slide by unnoticed when you're ten feet tall and twenty feet long! I've become a Dilophosaurus, and it's up to me to help Bertram Phillips fight J.D. Harms and save the future. This is my first day at Wetherford Junior High, and I'm already out of time. *Way* out!

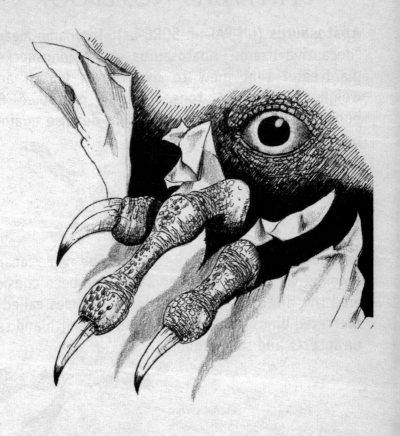

BERTRAM'S
NOTEBOOK

BERTRAM'S NOTEBOOK

Apatosaurus (uh-PAT-uh-SORE-us): The name means "deceptive lizard." Apatosaurus was a long-necked plant-eater that grew to 69 feet in length and weighed up to 24 tons. Its tail contained 82 bones and was used like a whip in defense against predators.

Apatosaurus

Archaeopteryx (ar-kee-OP-tur-iks): The name means "ancient wing." Archaeopteryx has long been considered the first bird, and it is also sometimes called a feathered dinosaur. It was two feet in length and fed on insects and small animals.

Archaeopteryx

Brontosaurus (BRON-tuh-SORE-us): The original name given to the sauropod Apatosaurus, later discarded by the scientific community. The term is still commonly used outside paleontological circles to refer to a variety of long-necks.

Carcharodontosaurus (kar-KAR-uh-DON-tuh-SORE-us): The name means "shark-toothed lizard." This dinosaur was a bipedal meat-eater with features like those of Allosaurus and Tyrannosaurus. A recently discovered specimen in this family sported an unusual and frightening scissor-shaped jaw. It was 45 feet long, 5 feet of which was skull.

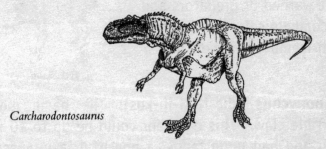

Carcharodontosaurus

Carnivores (KAR-nuh-vorz): Meat-eating animals.

Compsognathus (komp-sog-NAY-thus): The name means "elegant jaw." Compsognathus was a small meat-eater ranging from two to four feet in length. Weighing only six pounds, Compsognathus used its lightweight frame and incredible speed to catch small animals for food.

Compsognathus

Corythosaurus (kuh-RITH-uh-SORE-us): The name means "helmet lizard." One of the best-known duck-billed dinosaurs, Corythosaurus was a plant-eater that grew up to 33 feet long and had a high, hollow, bony head crest. Scientists believe that Corythosaurus could use their crests to make sounds that warned of predators and to communicate in other ways with members of their herds.

Corythosaurus

Deinonychus (die-NON-ih-kus): The name means "terrible claw." This dinosaur could be up to 10 feet long and had large fangs, a powerful jaw, muscular legs, and a retractable scythe-like claw on the second toe of each foot. Commonly known as "raptors," Deinonychus were fast and agile and usually hunted in packs to take down large prey.

Dilophosaurus (die-LOH-fuh-SORE-us): The name means "two-ridge lizard." Called "the terror of the early Jurassic," Dilophosaurus was a lithe, 19-foot-long hunter with a long tail. Two fragile semicircular crests rose from the head.

Dilophosaurus

Herbivores (HUR-bih-vorz): Plant-eating animals.

Hypsilophodon (hip-suh-LOH-fuh-don): The name means "high-ridge tooth." This dinosaur was a small herbivore, only about four to seven feet in length, but it was very quick. It walked on its two strong back legs.

Invertebrates (in-VUR-tuh-braytz): Animals without backbones, such as jellyfish.

Jurassic (juh-RAS-ik): The second of three distinct periods in the Mesozoic Era. The Jurassic Period began approximately 208 million years ago and ended 144 million years ago.

Massospondylus (mas-oh-SPON-duh-lus): The name means "massive vertebra." Massospondylus was a 16-foot-long, plant-eating dinosaur that walked on all fours and had vicious thumb claws that could be used for defense or as tools.

Massospondylus

Mesozoic Era (mez-uh-ZOH-ik ER-uh): The age of dinosaurs, 245 million to 65 million years ago.

Microvenator (MIE-kroh-vih-NAY-tor): The name means "tiny hunter." It was a small carnivorous dinosaur that walked on its hind legs and had unusually long arms.

Pachycephalosaurus (pack-ih-SEF-uh-luh-SORE-us): The name means "thick-headed lizard." These plant-eaters used their domelike heads for defense, ramming opponents with them much like present-day mountain goats.

Paleontologist (pay-lee-un-TAHL-uh-jist): A scientist who studies the past through fossils.

Scissor-jaw: See Carcharodontosaurus.

Scutellosaurus (skoo-TEL-uh-SORE-us): This dinosaur was named after the hundreds of scutes (bony studs) along its body, which shielded the animal from attack. It could walk or run on all fours or balance on its hind legs using its tail. This small plant-eater was four feet long.

Scutellosaurus

Stegosaurus (STEG-uh-SORE-us): The name means "roof lizard," which comes from the bony plates that jutted upward from the neck, back, and upper tail. This plant-eater grew up to 29 feet long and weighed two tons. Its main defensive weapon against attack was its tail, armed with four to eight spikes, each three to four feet long. The tail could be used with force and speed because of the dinosaur's ability to pivot very quickly on its hind legs.

Stegosaurus

Syntarsus (sin-TAR-sus): The name means "fused ankle." It was a 10-foot-long bipedal meat-eater. It was also fast-moving and had a long, flexible neck and a hollow tail.

Vertebrates (VUR-tuh-braytz): Animals with backbones, such as fish, mammals, reptiles, and birds.

The world: The continents and the seas of the earth 150 million years ago were very different from those of today. The supercontinent Pangaea was breaking up during the Jurassic Period. The Atlantic Ocean was created from rifts in the continents. Volcanic activity raged along much of what is now the west coast of the United States. Africa began to split from South America. The region that is now India prepared to drift toward Asia. Climates were warm worldwide.

The World—Present Day

The World—150 Million Years Ago

SCOTT'S FAVORITE DINO SITES

(and Bertram has them bookmarked, too!)

DINOSAUR INTERPLANETARY GAZETTE
www.dinosaur.org
This site has everything! You'll find up-to-date information on the newest and coolest dinosaurs (check out DNN, the Dinosaur News Network); plenty of links, jokes, quotes, interviews with authors (like me!) and paleontologists, and contests; and much, much more! The Gazette is the winner of 22 Really Kewl Awards and is recommended by the National Education Association.

DINOSAUR WORLD
www.dinoworld.net
A "nature preserve" for hundreds of awesome life-size dinosaurs, located in Plant City, Florida, between Tampa and Orlando. I've never seen anything like it! Check it out on the Net, then go see it for yourself!

DINOTOPIA
www.dinotopia.com
I'm the author of four Dinotopia digest novels, *Windchaser*, *Lost City*, *Thunder Falls*, and *Sky Dance*. Dinotopia is one of my favorite places to visit. This is the official Web site of James Gurney's epic creation. Enter a world of wonder where humans and dinosaurs peacefully co-exist. Ask questions of Bix, post messages to fellow fans, and be sure to let Webmaster Brokehorn know that Scott at DINOVERSE sent you!

PREHISTORIC TIMES
members.aol.com/pretimes
This Web site offers information about the premier magazine for dinosaur enthusiasts around the world—published by DINOVERSE illustrator Mike Fredericks. For dinosaur lovers, aspiring dinosaur artists, and more!

ZOOMDINOSAURS.COM
www.zoomdinosaurs.com
A terrific resource for students. Lots of puzzles, games, information for writing dinosaur reports, classroom activities, an illustrated dinosaur dictionary, frequently asked questions, and fantastic information for dinosaur beginners.

• AUTHOR'S SPECIAL THANKS •

Thanks to Denise Ciencin, M.A., National Certified Counselor, for her many valued and wonderful contributions to this novel. For helping me to reconstruct the world of California 150 million years ago, thanks to paleontologists Richard Hilton, Professor, Department of Geology, Sierra College, Rocklin, California; Frank DeCourten, Professor, Department of Geology and Earth Sciences, Sierra College, Rocklin, California; Robert F. Walters, Paleontological Life Restoration Artist, American Museum of Natural History, New York City, New York; and Dr. Phillip J. Currie, Curator of Dinosaurs, Royal Tyrrell Museum of Palaeontology, Adjunct Associate Professor, University of Calgary, and Adjunct Professor, University of Saskatchewan, Canada.

Special thanks to Alice Alfonsi, my extraordinary editor, and all our friends at Random House, especially Kate Klimo, Cathy Goldsmith, Tanya Mauler, Mike Wortzman, Lisa Findlay, Artie Bennett, Jenny Golub, and Christopher Shea.

Final thanks to my incredible agent, Jonathan Matson.